Funeralopolis

FUNERALOPOLIS

DANIEL BEAUREGARD

Orbis Tertius Press

Alberta, Canada

Cover design and interior layout by Kimberley Palsat

ISBN: 978-1-0688637-0-7

ORBIS TERTIUS PRESS

Contents

Contents

A Terrified Rabbit
(with its Ears in the Wind)

As I stepped out the door, I perceived a great cloud overhead in the shape of the head of a rabbit. It was a terrified rabbit, its ears in the wind, pulled back behind its head. A terrified rabbit with its ears in the wind. I thought about the times we'd collect the fallen pine needles, building a bed of them on the basement floor, imagining birds all around us. We met there at the end of each day, that space being but a small part inside of us, quiet in comparison to everything else. The days when I'd go hunting, trudging through the knee-high snow in a daze, directionless, passing the time counting the rhythm that populated my steps. If I was offbeat, I'd stop and look, then continue. Then stop and look again, then continue hesitatingly. I'd stop and start a hundred times until finally I'd make up my mind, stopping and sitting right there in the snow. If only you could've seen me, you'd either have respected me or perhaps have been ashamed. I'd not begrudge you either one. Those times I'd sit and think well into the day, until the sun rose high into the sky and my ass got wet and frozen.

Since it won't matter much now, I'll tell you. I've never once, in all my life, caught a rabbit. Those days of hunting were full of aimless wandering, smelling the things I encountered in the forest. When the sun began to dip in the afternoon, I'd hurry to the butcher at the foot of the mountain and buy two rabbits. Always two for some reason, although one was more than enough. In those days, we both ate sparingly. The butcher kept my secret faithfully. I think so at least, for you never made mention of it, and surely if the butcher had said, *Your tall man came in only yesterday and purchased two rabbits from me,* you would have certainly made mention of it, or asked whether I had been there that week, to the butcher, I mean, or at the very least found it strange and something to make note of. But if you noted it, you never said. Or he never said. So, on the days where you went in my stead to purchase whatever small vittles we needed— for it was I who bought the rabbits—you never returned with a single question. I loved both of you for that. On the days where I couldn't leave the bed, it was a blessing that my shameful secret was kept. Perhaps you knew—you know now at least—or you've always known, keeping any mention of it to yourself out of love. But what matters most is my speaking it out loud, now, to you, upon the forest air. This forest and its humble creatures. This forest and its multitude of scampering, humble creatures. This forest and all its darkened refuges. This forest, with its darkened corners scattered beneath bushes, between the snow. This forest and its beds of softened pine needles. This forest and its rabbits. This forest's rabbits, which always elude me, which will always elude me.

It's a shame all our children are dead, because I'm sure they would have grown to enjoy us. Well, perhaps you, anyway. But now you're gone, too. Now you're gone too—they're all gone—

A Terrified Rabbit (With its Ears in the Wind)

and I'm walking to find help. I'm walking through this forest before your body is frozen stiff. I'm walking to find help before the day is at its end and the chill night freezes your blue limbs into a gesture I can never forget. I've finally climbed out of bed and am walking after finding you there on the floor, painfully crumpled up like a dead spider, your limbs contorted exactly like the dead spiders we'd always find on the windowsill of the kitchen. I'm walking through this forest full of rabbits, and I'm ashamed that it's taken this to bring me out of my self-imposed exile. I am sorry. It is true what you always said: the fresh air does a mind good. Therefore, I'm walking in the fresh air. It is doing me good, except for the fact that you are back there, dead and crumpled up on the floor, just like a spider. Fresh air does a body good if it's alive. But when dead, it freezes you quickly into a confused and horrified gesture.

One would think a life spent living inside their mind would teach them something useful. I've tried almost every goddamn thing at this point, even a deadfall. Still, not once have I managed to catch a rabbit. I chuck shit at them, exasperated, after everything else has failed—everything. I've thrown stones at them—everything. But it never seems to make a difference. This forest has everything a good forest has and everything a good forest should. This forest has birds that are often quite loud, although now they are quiet because they are nesting. This forest has birds and so many rabbits, some of which are nesting too. There are so many, it's almost unbelievable, but it's true. They're here among us. Among me, as I trudge through the knee-high snow in a daze. Is it because I don't know how to kill them? Is that, perhaps, why these rabbits exist in this forest in such multitudes? Each morning, all the butcher does is raise his awning and stretch, then whistle, and all the rabbits rush into his shop. This is a lie. Or perhaps not. But I imagine it this way: that the butcher does this each morning, and that it must be a lie, for I've made it up right here on the spot, my knees growing wet. It's a shame that you and our children are dead, especially since I've finally risen, looked the sun in the eye, and spoken my secret into the freezing air. No one's here to watch it float upward. I am trying to find help in a wood full of rabbits I cannot catch. I also—it pains me and makes me terribly ashamed to admit—am unbearably hungry, and in all honesty, I may have risen and left the house more for fear of starving in a cold, rabbitless hut than to arrange some sort of requiem for you, my dead and faithful wife.

If you are here alongside me anywhere in this forest, could you give me a sign? It can be almost anything, really. I only ask that it not be a rabbit. It's so quiet; it could be almost anything though, really. Even a tuft of snow falling off a branch in the treetops would be enough. It's not enough for me to simply wish or really believe you're here beside me; I need something more. Even dead, I'm still asking. I pause here momentarily to see if you'll reciprocate. So beautiful as it is in the forest. Nothing will really change if I simply catch my breath for a moment. It's still early in the day, after all. The sun isn't even really that high in the sky. I plop down. A small poof falls from the treetops to the frozen forest floor, almost floating in its genuine softness. Was that you? It wasn't, was it? I feel like a sign, whatever it would be, would be much more pronounced. Isn't that right? I mean, you knew me well enough—know me well enough—to make it something a little more pronounced, more assertive, perhaps. After all, a sign is a sign, but one still really needs to be able to determine with some certainty whether it was divine or simply an act of nature. Of course, one could argue that nature is divine. That aside, I think a tuft of snow falling off a branch should really be on the list—the list of things I don't want as a sign. I'm sorry, but no tufts of snow falling off branches or rabbits either, I'm afraid. That really should be it, I think.

You appeared only a moment earlier, as a rabbit, I think, then scampered off into the woods. I'm sitting here in the deep snow. It has melted slightly and formed a cradle around my body. During winter, if one is quiet enough in the forest, a grinding, clacking type of sound surrounds you if one breathes softly. It's the snow flexing itself upon the things that surround you, flexing itself upon the things it surrounds. It sounds like hard, icy snow falling very quietly, or like tossing sand onto sand or out into the wind. It makes one want to hold their breath and marvel at the beauty and quietude of the forest. I do it now. I hold my breath for as long as I can before letting out a long, frosty sigh that finds its way into the treetops and dissipates. It's better to breathe deeply when one has the chance and to sit for a time while the sun is still high. Even if my ass is getting wet, it won't really be bothersome once I begin again. Another tuft of snow falls from high above in the treetops, landing right on top of me—on my head. It takes a moment to realize what's happened. Once I do, I rub the snow out of my eyes with a chuckle and open them wide. Before me, a rabbit emerges out of the bushes. We sit completely still.

We hold completely still. It had to be this way, really. Now we realize that it really did have to be this way: you, most certainly here. Right. It serves me right, indeed. The man who's never trapped or caught a rabbit. You are really here—or are there, rather—the rabbit in front of me. This forest is full of surprises. The sun is still high in the sky, and we remain motionless. It's so comfortable here, even if my ass is wet. It really does serve us right. You, as a rabbit; this forest. Everything really. I'm struck with the idea that perhaps if we stay here—stay still—long enough, you or the rabbit, or whatever soul really inhabits this humble creature directly in front of me, will mistake me for a bush.

Perhaps this ignorant creature will be unfortunate enough to mistake me for a place of refuge—a harmless fixture—and come close enough so it falls within my grasp. If I remain completely still, it could be possible. I could really snatch it up if it came within arm's reach. It shouldn't be so hard. What a sign you've shown us. I realize now that this is, with certainty, a divine revelation. The sun is still fairly high, so really, we're not pressed for time. I asked for no rabbits, but since you've forgiven us, I'll forgive this oversight. It was—in fact—both of the items on the list of non-signs, but really, it's no matter.

There you are—as the sun hits the forest floor—illuminated, so small and slender. We're here together and I'm sure it must be you. We're here together, really—the two of us—nervous but unafraid. We remain completely still. I'm remaining motionless, and you are paused, tense, alert like any other rabbit. This could be our only chance, I think. You are alert like any other rabbit would be, so remaining completely motionless is essential. I try to use our energy, our love, to draw you toward me. There is time yet. The sun is somewhat further along in its path, but no matter. Our ass is hardly wet. We're unbearably hungry, yet light. We feel light, like if we didn't need to eat, we wouldn't have to, which is somewhat inconsistent with our earlier statement of unbearable hunger and rather hard to explain.

The head of a rabbit changes into the head of a horse. The head of a rabbit. The head of a horse. There are now few clouds over-head. The sky is a crystal blue, poking through the pines. Now my ass is getting wet; I can really feel it. But it's so comfortable here. Just to pause for a moment. Neither of us has moved. Well, that's not entirely true. You've moved very slightly to pluck the berries off the tree in front of us. I, however, have remained

A Terrified Rabbit (With its Ears in the Wind)

motionless. The snow has melted and formed a cradle or throne around my body, and I'm nestled snugly inside of it, as if it were always made for us. It's like it existed just beneath the snow in exactly the right place where I've chosen to sit. Now I make an effort to move and shield my eyes from the sun for a moment. I try doing so in a way where I move as little as possible, but it's difficult. My limbs are stiff. The snow has melted and formed this cradle around me, and I struggle to shield the sun from my eyes momentarily. It's quite high up now. You haven't moved much yet, just to nibble, and that's all.

Now my ass really is beginning to get wet. But it's so comfortable here that I'm hesitant to move. It's so comfortable, but I'm also hesitant to move because of the fact that you are in front of me. The sun is glinting through the treetops and is well on its way now. I try to remain motionless, only moving slightly to block its rays and get a better look at you. My god, I hadn't noticed, but my ass really is quite wet. There you are in front of me, nibbling the berries on a bush I can't identify. It really is you; I can still hardly believe it. If I wasn't afraid you'd run off and leave me—although I'd deserve it—I'd jump up and down for joy. But my limbs have really gotten quite stiff, and it's a struggle to keep the sun from my eyes. Perhaps it's all this motionless movement, this trying to be precise, that's gotten me all disjointed, rigid. At least I'm here where it's comfortable—my throne of melting snow—even if my ass is wet. Are you coming closer now? It seemed for a moment that you were coming closer. Wait, come closer. It isn't so late yet. If you're afraid, we can wait until the time is right. I had begun to put my arm—which was still in the air to block the light from the sun—back down. But I've stopped, and I remain motionless. We are looking at each other. So small and slender. You could come right up to me now. You really could.

You've moved a little closer toward me. I told you, you could come right up to me now. I've managed to slowly lower our rigid arm without startling you away. You stand there somewhat alert —so slender—with your paws rustling through the branches to pick away the berries from the front end of the bush. Do you finally recognize me? Is that why you've come closer? Have you decided I'm not a threat? Shit. This throne of snow is really making my ass wet, but you're almost within reach. Besides, once we get moving, I'll thaw out quickly; it'll be like we never stop-ped. You've picked and eaten all the berries on the back of the shrub and are making your way toward the front. It's comfortable enough here, although it's beginning to get quite cold. My limbs are stiff as a board from all this motionless movement, this quiet precision, ha ha. I still can't believe you're here. I'm all disjointed and rigid, like I'm stuck to this throne of ice—snow, I mean. Well, it could be ice now, who knows.

You've definitely come closer, almost within reach now. At least we're quite comfortable; my ass is probably totally soaked by now. If you could only see, ha ha. But you're right there. Are you ashamed? It's all this motionless movement, but because of this, you've come even closer, and closer still. I can smell the wetness of your fur. There's no longer any need to block the sunlight. I try to raise my arm to reach for you. It's still quite stiff—everything is—maybe even more so than before. A sign is a sign, of course, though. Besides, once we're up and moving again, it'll be like we've never stopped. Isn't it better to breathe deeply when one has the chance? But now we hold our breath, for you are really right there in front of me. My limbs are quite stiff, but I move my arm almost imperceptibly to try and—this really should be it, I think—yes, we've almost gotten there. You've come so much closer. The smell of the wetness of your fur—it's like, it's like the smell of the forest. Probably like berries or something more inarticulate. Fuck, just a little more. My limbs are being

A Terrified Rabbit (With its Ears in the Wind)

stubborn. You're right there, right in front of us. I told you you could really come right up to me now—all this motionless movement—and you have. So slender, if we could only—fuck—

There Was a Place in Our Neck Where Meaning Once Stood

—A piece of metal has burnt its way into my chest—

A piece of metal—the smell—a bullet has burnt its way into my chest. Or something. The forest has burnt its way into my life. No. Something has pissed its breath into my lungs. Perhaps. I hit the ground with a thud, and they trample me. Who could blame them? Hit the ground with a thud, traced hooves into my snout, my muzzle side whole body, punched-through flesh. The frenzy. Trampled me; who could blame them? Far off, the forest melts behind them; leaves scatter. I sink into the ground. We are returning. My limbs thrust forward. I place them. Hooves. Find little purchase in the rotten muck. We persist, find a foothold, and lift. Unsure, we chatter our bones together and collapse. Our backward knees. It isn't good. The forest enemy. We raise ourselves. We slip and the forest finds us on its rotten floor again— the vegetal leaves that smell so close to sour but not quite. We feel ourself being dragged into something. Or slipping. Slipping? No.

Spilling. Escaping. Voiding ourself. Voiding outwards. In the forest long ago, before moss upon the bones of the ancient, the air running born, we were alone. We were never running, really. Or were we always? Where did we come from, and why are we here now? Born in the air. Sinking into death—the forest floor. It wraps its vegetal glow; surrounds us. We hear far off; the smells rent the air. Far off where our others run, the air struggles to heave them up. Perhaps the forest thins where the herd runs now. No? Perhaps it is I who will help them escape. All slowing, I move myself further into the trees. I will draw them to me, the hunters. I scrape at the ground in progress. Far off, something like night, edging in to make it fade. Receding. The trees are no longer beautiful, but terrifying. Stripped of necessity: barren, charred. We have been successful in making it this far. Huddle now. Make it to the edge of nothing, no. Make it behind an area in the ground. The ground is sinking. We are falling away from the forest. It's looming now, darkness. It is dark where we're going—perhaps dark where we've been. Dew a remembrance: something one can simply smell and feel at home. If only. I cry, but it bubbles away from my throat like the farting ground. There was a place in my neck where meaning once stood. The forest, the smell—all at once, it overcomes our spirit. Will we remember this once death consumes us? The forest, the smell. The hunt was like it was. Forever. The hunt forever running, chasing into the air. They will fall upon me then. The hunt. The makers of flight. For us? Perhaps they are the reason... Always running. The smell rents the air. Blowing apart the bark of those that live inside us. Our sisters born. Our brothers born. Blown apart eventually, when the air refuses them. Heavy we sink—taken down—the vegetal state of our bodies. For when we stop running, we die. Or, no? When will we die? I am dying. The stagnant water fills my hoof prints, tracing a trail back to when the dew was sweet. Back to the days we were a part of once. We were born into the herd, we think. How did we make it this far?

If there was ever a place to run, it would be backwards, not forwards. Perhaps they've found the place where the forest ends. There are stones there, many coloured; so said the ancient one—our guide—before the hunt hacked his storied greatness into moss. Left upon the ground, grown green—not bleach—the sun forever divided upon the forest floor. We have worn our life apart. Pull the bark and sniff the sap; may it pay for us. The hunt comes closer. Twigs beneath. Twigs, the forest floor. We lift ourselves up: head, then neck, then body, then limb; we can hardly tell from life painting, sodden ground below, our life once red when the sun went down. The forest at night. The forest at down. The hunt approaches, and we smell their sour musk. Piss of death, clink of iron. Leaves dead tremble the forest floor; kick themselves closer to our death. We try to rise, slip, try again. It's leaving us. Our stories float above our head in darkness. No. Our vision fails; glows. No. Comes back, now blue. Sunlight? I smell a sister in the air, one met long ago—the ground. They wear her piss to drive us mad. I cannot away. We have prepared. Come, melt my bones with moss; bog them up. The air bears the smell of death times a thousand. Piss-bottled addlers. Green the dusk. Spare nothing. Ritual. Tie coils around the heart of space. Place us near the running water. They lift us up. Sideways. Upside down. Our moulting head brushes the forest floor. We paint with life. The sun goes down. Our fake sisters crunch along beside us, and chatter floods our softened ears. The air no longer cares. It's our fault, not hers. Never hers. Stories flood our nostrils. We remember, then forget. Our limbs. Hooves clack, tied together. The forest floor. Antlers. No moss. No. Never did we think it could turn that way, did we think our piss; we are covered in our piss. It mats the fur and dribbles off our snout. The sun is upside down. Green disappearing. Perhaps their flight has found the edge. The hunt. Is there a flock of them, or have they all fallen upon me? Beneath us, they have placed an item to catch our leakage. Powerless to snort. Slip the life out of it; we're ready. Come out then.

Come then. Stop rustling direction. Forward leave. Come finish it. Scraping toward us. Sight depends on water we watch fill hoof prints; the mud spackle. Much like hunger, this feeling. Or no? And then it comes, glinting. We wish our brothers and sisters luck. The forest, green, the smell falls upon us. We struggle to huff and watch our breath disappear, the sun disappear, the forest, our smell. The hunt—the knife—pierces us close by our musky parts—a history—comes scaling down, opening us up. Iron wets the forest floor; everything spills out. The rotting leaves. What is this death? The smell of death. The smell of shit.

—A fly finds a resting place upon our rump—

After Kafka

I'd like to return this mirror if I may, says a man, struggling with a large mirror. What seems to be the problem with this particular mirror? The clerk in the complaints department asks without looking up.

I can't see myself in it; that's the problem. The more I look at it, the more I realize I could never see myself in such a mirror. No ... no, not this one; it's just not possible, and it certainly wasn't cheap.

The salesperson seems taken aback, then vaguely gestures that he'll return in a moment, shuffling off into a darker corner of the office.

A strong, colossal man with a fiery red beard emerges from the shadows and takes the place where the previous clerk was sitting, the chair groaning beneath his weight.

Now, what seems to be the problem?

As I explained to your associate, this mirror doesn't work.

What? Doesn't work, you say?

The man scratches his beard in thought, then stands up from behind the desk, crossing to the front of the room where the other man stands nervously, still struggling to hold the heavy mirror.

Prop it up there—the other man says, pointing to a nearby chair—let's have a look.

The nervous man props the mirror up against the chair.

Both stand back and look.

After a moment, the man with the fiery beard exclaims, By Christ, you're right; my head's been cut clean off!

The heavy mirror then suddenly slides off the chair onto the floor, shattering into a multitude of pieces. Horrified, the nervous man gets down on his hands and knees, hurriedly picking up the shards until he freezes—each one bears his face in varying degrees, but none is the precise one he is looking for.

VHS tape /
The Invisible Man

Gazing at himself. Nothing. Nude. Naked in the mirror, but nothing. No one knows. No hat or penis. No briefcase floating in the air. A VHS tape levitates off the table in the corner, floats to the middle of the room above a chair, then is thrust down forcefully upon its edge, cracking open like a broken egg. Its film is extracted, the empty husk of the cassette tossed onto the floor. Slowly, he winds it. Slowly. Then the crown of the head. Forehead. Face—its muted contours—materializes. He continues like this: smashing tape cassettes, bringing his body into place. The best he can do with such little notice.

Static of Something Frying

You left the eggs on again.

Pressing on Your Eyelids

To be frank, I don't even remember in the slightest what a kaleidoscope looks like. But I can imagine it well. Jagged coloured edges mirrored, heft in twain. Something poetic about its plasticity, or how it looks plastic. Or crumpled tinfoil. Aluminium insides bouncing off of plastic. Better to stare into the sun, then close your eyes quickly. A convex mirror: the iris. Without it, what then?

A Fly

His wings, like static; I forgot about the eggs on again, the fly, in the hope of perching upon something rotten or rotting, or finding an item to puke on at the very least. Staying stationary above a frying pan, his sound mixes with the popping grease while the man adjacent to the burner has a heart attack. He reaches for his telephone but freezes mid-motion, awkwardly holding his arm in the air. The noise remains, but it's much more pronounced now and we wonder: is this something that could possibly happen on a daily basis? We can hear, arpeggiating through it all, the struggling little gasps for air as though made by an out-of-breath chipmunk.

Unidentifiable Architecture
(angled lines and chiselled spaces)

Something is constructed, but we're unsure of what it is, much like corners in a dream; hastily put together; shapes; lines; unclear angles (if they can be that way). A looming matter of construction. Before us, but somehow somewhere else. Everywhere we place our hands, the spackling just seems too thick—too much to ever be able to get away with in any sharp sense of reality. It is a house; we are made to enter it.

Bungalow with Carport Being Attacked by Other Homes

It is a house; we are made to enter it even as it is being devoured by other homes, suburban architecture subtly masquerading as the creeping vines that line its walkways. Wisteria. Carport: gone. Ivy. Windows: gone. The car out front: gone. Sinking backwards. If it had another storey, perhaps things would be different, but the bungalow is peeking from behind the curtains of Time. Our old neighbour, Ted, used to have BBQs on his roof just because he could. He's dead now. So are we.

Falling into the Sea

It suddenly falls into the sea. Us. We. The bungalow. Time and everything else, sounding with one sharp snap. We look for sand dollars while the bungalow pretends to be a jellyfish, but it can't float—it never could—so it fashions its sensible red-brick chimney into a periscope, lobbing night tables at whomever comes too close. We built the house on a precipice with the intention of it someday falling into the sea. We built it to watch it edge slowly off the cliff each year, like an old couple in Cape Cod, timing our mistakes to the faithful wash of a lighthouse in the distance, the body of which could never be seen through the fog. Every year, we inched a little more until ... here we are. O'Neil would be proud, or perhaps devastated. If he'd've pushed himself a little further, the stage would have flooded.

Sweating Doorknobs

sweating doorknobs

/swɛt/**ŋg**/ - /ˈdɔːnʋb/

1. A breakfast cereal for giants, enjoyed in times long since passed.
2. What a house might do when it has a hot date.
3. What a date might do when it has a hot house.

Look through water

Sometimes it's like opening your eyes underwater, but it looks like the surface of it for some reason. It's like opening your eyes underwater to stare at the surface of the water— the way the light's reflected in ripples, dancing from one area to the next like heat lightning skipping around in the sky. It's not dangerous, but the power remains: like falling into a Jello mould, which reminds one of: children and the infirm, looking down into an indoor pool at the elderly, or being wheeled through memory; such sanitizing thoughts bubble to the surface.

Cleanliness to what? Some believe they're owed cleanliness until the very end; others think they owe a tidy death to those they loved. Needle in the dark and a shot in the ass.

Flip a nurse on her back and watch the monitor go from bright green to red to off-the-charts. In the exercise pool, access is restricted to those with the relevant clearance. The orderlies shrink back when the jets turn on; they provide a soothing lullaby for the dementia patients; they're imagining blowing bubbles in chocolate milk, farting underwater.

The orderlies watch the chloronic spume gather and reflect their eyes. Thousands of them, like a fly's eye. Or maggots in the larval stage. Age is death, and death is endless, like the surface of the pool, or, for some reason, like a psychomanteum.

A thousand fingers watching a woman undress

Each one is a mæstro, a baton, a thing to wield. These are not fingers; are they fingers?

When one self departs, the other slowly follows, like a spirit shadow

Like slicing yourself into perfect segments, which is the true self—the one that leads or the one that follows? Or splitting yourself into three segments or four, like an exploded skull. And if we could only explode in such a way, the world would be better off for it. When our spirit shadow tears itself away from the flesh, from memory, and from synapses, it guides us toward our primal issues.

Without the body, the mind is free to face its problems head-on; work out the best solution without a worry of tearing away some part of itself. Meeting things head-on without a head on, later hitching a ride out on a moonbeam.

Visiting every locale from high above, with the scale of others—of buildings and people and places and landmarks—seriously diminished.

Birds fly south for the winter because they've grown so tired of industry; it's been that way for centuries, but the labcoats keep getting it wrong.

Splicing experience into place

The sharper the pen knife, the easier it will be to penetrate the skull, where we're going.

Inside the skull is a greyish mass of cauliflower where our styles are kept, which we need to train to combat atrophy. It can be eaten to sponge up its powers or the powers of another. Also used in rituals, the cauliflower is an important staple in curry dishes the world over.

Some people have brains, others have cauliflower.

I was talking about brains at one point but shifted focus.

If executed perfectly, with a pen knife, you can slice, quite properly, something altogether new that can combine the skin/varying attributes into a bodily film. It is the latest and greatest form of special effects; the director poured all of his sweat and blood into it—that kinda thing, you know?

Those higher up in the film industry have always been cutthroats, so why not work with what you got?

Put together the best of everything; you can craft a masterpiece.

With so much lightning there's little use for lamps nowadays

In our home, there's so much lightning that there's little use for lamps nowadays. It's true they can come in handy for decorative purposes, but not much else. Plus, there's always the danger of leaving one on for days when we go under—it's a fire hazard, Danny says—so we prefer to operate by the light of the moon and the electric sky. Uncle Bob drives golf balls off the roof of the bungalow each night to tempt fate. He will soon be struck dead; there's no doubt about it, but he's vigilant. If only he'd tried as hard to keep his first marriage together, he'd likely have a larger spot on the couch. We frequent the yard, playing games. Although everyone's an adult, it's summertime, so it's OK to let loose now and then. We play tag in the yard and are only allowed to move each time the lightning lights up the sky. It can often go on for hours without a champion. All the while, Uncle Bob screams "Fore!" from the roof of the carport, and Maisy's inside somewhere, crying or trying to decide if she should leave. She could go and never come back, for all I care.

Many of the lines (piping, walls, etc.) seem to have remained mostly intact, despite all the ideas being blown away.

Have you ever built a house out of toothpicks? It's like that, but bigger and much more costly.

The Invisible Man returns donning a tight-fitting VHS tape dress that accentuates his hourglass physique.

Classic sequel.

Floaters change into strands of genetic mutations or evidence

On the beach, alone, with white sand surrounding me, I was attacked by what I thought was a fly. Everywhere my head turned, a flicker would recede into the periphery before I could get a clear look. I continued this exercise fruitlessly for what seemed to be days. Eventually, I plopped down on the ground and gave up. Then I saw them in front of me, like tiny little spots or what you might see through a microscope before adjusting the magnification. They've stayed with me ever since.

A living Cornell box

Lighting under the stairs to cast ample shadows onto the wall: a person, walking up, then down, then up again, nonstop. Walls made from balsa wood crack and break easily but can be easily repaired, so it's a wash. What we want to focus on here is the pain and anxiety Cornell portrays by washing the dishes in the kitchen white. When the Mothman spies on people, he sees two sets of curtains and 40 of the same person, all in an instant.

The Courtyard & the Castle Keep

-after Julio Cortázar's *Carta a una señorita en París*

We'd wandered into the courtyard of a dimly lit castle at dusk, drawn by a man gesticulating wildly from a keep far up above. It was difficult to tell if he was trying to get our attention or waving his arms in the air for another reason, but the movement was curious enough to draw our eyes. We sat on a stone bench in the courtyard below, gazing up at where we thought his arms might extend once more. But, the moment we sat down, his arms quickly disappeared from view. A moment later, a horrid, retching noise began—echoing as if amplified by a loudspeaker—from the spires high above. At first, we're unsure of the sound and fear for our lives, then we cover our ears with our hands and cower beneath the stone bench, the only noticeable fixture in the courtyard. The noise continues (in a moment, we realize it wouldn't be stopping any time soon). Once our ears adjusted to the nuisance and we realized we weren't in any immediate danger, we crawled out from beneath the bench and continued gazing upwards. After some time, we discerned a renewed sense of movement. The gentleman was back at the window. The retching resumed forcefully and then stopped, almost as suddenly as it began. A white object was thrust into the air and fell toward us at an alarming rate. We barely had enough time to sidestep before it hit the paving stones of the courtyard with a sickening thud. It began moving awkwardly, dragging itself toward us upon its broken limbs.

In the courtyard below the castle, the dusk is perpetual—only just enough light to make out the silhouettes of certain things but never solidify them into being, at least not from a distance of more than a few meters. We wonder how we could have possibly managed to have seen the man who attracted us in the first place, but then we quickly dismiss the thought. Since the first rabbit fell, there have been many others, all different shapes and sizes. No matter how damaged they are from the impact, each one seems to have the ability to drag their broken body back and forth in front of us, on display. We watch one with a broken neck try to lift its head to look at us, and, disgusted, we forcefully kick it away and watch it slide along the ground, pushing its way through the jumble of mutilated rabbits huddled on the other side of the courtyard. Every few minutes or so, another joins its ranks. At first, it appeared as though they'd been damaged on their way down from the keep, nicking the side of the castle—a brick or two—before slapping to the ground. Now, we're not so sure. Some are missing limbs that appear to have been amputated; others are blind, repeatedly bumping into things that obstruct their path. Some have been flayed. Each that hobbles toward us is covered in a septic, bright-green goo; bile perhaps?

The rabbits have finally stopped falling from the castle keep, and the man gesticulates wildly once again. We raise our voice in an attempt at communication, but either he doesn't hear us or he chooses to ignore our pleas. A grating noise is heard, and four large pillars emerge from the ground and surround the courtyard, each bearing a different symbol etched deeply into the stone from which they're carved. The first, a crudely drawn matchstick man with a bird above his head. The second, a roaring fire; the third, Pan, or some other half-man, half-goat creature. The fourth, a mirror reflecting our true nature. This is a surprise. Our image is carved deeply into the rock but also moves as we move, shifting in space as we admire ourselves. We reach out, fingering the smooth surface. At the moment our fingertips touch it, several large steel grates emerge from the ground. Before we realize what's happening, it's too late; any existing exit from the court-yard has been blocked. Above us is an unbreakable grate with mesh squares so small we're unable to scale it with our fingers.

Now we congregate with the mutilated rabbits in the corner. To pass the time—for it seems like we've been here for days, if not more—we've begun naming each of the monstrosities by their persisting maladies (The Flayed & Mighty, Hoichi the Earless, The Wink, The Scream, Oliver Head). Shortly after the grates had been drawn, the sky began to lighten, slightly but noticeably. Then the birds came, attracted by the flavour of the wind tunnelling its way out of the courtyard. Now we understand. Whether we were part of this plan or an unfortunate interloper remains a mystery. Our only solace is the small satchel of pepper-corns stashed in the breast pocket of our coat. We grab a few and pop them in our mouth, grinding them with our teeth, feeling the pleasant, numbing sensation spread down the back of our throat and the pockets of our cheeks, waiting for a change in atmosphere.

The sun has now risen fully into the sky, driving the birds into a frenzy. They begin to tear at the grate overhead, the clacking of their beaks reaching a deafening proportion. In a moment of inspiration—an effort to end our torture—we rise, slowly, moving toward the pillar that bears our true nature. Smiling at ourselves on its smooth surface, we watch the reflection grin back at us in glistening clarity, then walk over to the pillar with the matchstick man and the bird above his head and draw our hand across its polished surface. A low, juddering sound erupts, and the grate above our head retracts. The birds and noise and everything cease for a moment, and the courtyard is bathed in unimaginable silence. But now they're upon us—and the rabbits. From the corner of a blood-flecked eye, we see the man in the keep staring down at us, the mad king, throwing crumbs to his courtesans.

Golemitos

We'll never make it out of here alive; it's impossible. Each day, we use the rangefinder embedded in our right eye to focus on the pores of our skin, zooming in until they look like the little holes in Swiss cheese that have bubbled and burst away, forgotten. We'll never make it—you ought to listen to us. We know for sure. We focus intently on one of the holes until it becomes clear in our optic viewfinder, readying our tweezers for extraction—the first time we saw this, we were fucking amazed—and just as if we were playing Operation®, we reach in slowly, without touching the sides of the pores. If the tweezers come in too strong or too loud, it spooks the little versions of ourselves burrowed deep within. It's like this: everybody has more than a million pores, and inside each lives a tiny golem tied to a string called Destiny. When you squeeze a blackhead, it's considered murder. Here's one: see the tiny thread attached to it as we pull it out and place it on the windowsill? No, that's right. Of course you don't; you're not fitted with optical implants, but trust me, it's there. Based on the stethoscope, mask, and tiny white gloves, this must be a doctor, a surgeon perhaps. Another one: here. It's a lawyer; see his little hat? The next is simply a newly formed idea of success. Plug into our temple port. Now there, see? There are three tiny versions of ourselves standing next to each other on the windowsill. Look what happens when the thread of Destiny is torn or broken. With our small pliers we snip the doctor's thread with a flick of the wrist. For a moment nothing happens, then the tiny doctor drops to his knees, hands around his head, screaming something incomprehensible. A millisecond later, he bursts into flames; his ashes thicken and grow like black snake fireworks, extending across the sill, then breaking off and plummeting to the floor below. Watch what happens when I open the window and let the lawyer out. (At this point, I should also mention that the thread of Destiny will stretch as far as need be but become ever more fragile the further away the golemito's body gets from its host.) Watch! The lawyer's looking left and right. He's scaling the wall cautiously to the ground below. Now he's down. But he's only managed to take several steps. Here comes a masked assailant. My goodness, he's got a little black ski mask on and everything. I don't think the lawyer's going to get too far today. We watch as the masked figure drives a knife into his heart. The thread of Destiny is severed and burns toward us like a tiny fuse back to the pore from which it came. Next up is the newly-formed idea of success, which, in theory, should have a better chance in the open air because it's still abstract. Let's crack the window. See how it floats upwards into the air for a moment, then totally deflates? It's turning the colour of jade now and crumbling away into nothing. Starting to get the picture? What's that? You think you'll try it anyway, despite my protests? Fine with me. After all, it's your life, not mine. Go ahead if you want. There you go, right out the window there—watch the ledge. Look at you! We're amazed.

You're right there in front of us—outside—and it appears nothing's happening. You're sure you're not feeling something—anything? Really? Great, you say? Never better? You really feel all right? Then perhaps we've miscalculated. Yes, it would be good to get some fresh air. But are you sure it's safe? Believe us, we'd like nothing more than to leave. You're absolutely positive? All right, then. Eventually we've got to learn to trust one another; why not now? Here, help me—yes, that's it. Let me just get my leg up and over, and—ah, there we go. Here we are. Yes, indeed, it is refreshing—very refreshing. But just a moment, we seem to be caught on something. It's right behi—Oh Christ!, we shout, watching in horror as the window slams shut, severing a thick piece of twine. A little wick from our bottom illuminates the night in blinding fashion, then poof! We're right back where we started; this child's life, it's often inescapable.

Berrigan's Eras

Berrigan's ears whistle like pipe cleaners in the wind; a head too big for his body, forepaws fluffy and concise. Passing by a window, a man can't resist holding something so small in his hands. They found him from the ground floor of Cortázar's apartment building, somehow still alive, flip-flopping about. I walked to the patio and slipped on the leavings underfoot, hardened and small like tiny ball bearings; something was nibbling nearby, but I couldn't say what. Early mornings filled with exhaust; a faint smell of straw—musky, earthy, and pastoral —lingers in the early morning, although there was only sprawl below. I could have never kept him. I imagined every rabbit I saw was part of an untold fairy tale; a familiar, because they're fast and so hard to catch. Corralling Berrigan was next to impossible. Days seemed like weeks, like months, like years. Nibbling nearby, troubling my sleep. This was not the life I imagined, I thought with a sigh, wondering if we could elope somewhere to spend the days and nights in the solitude of a hollowed oak.

Perhaps then, perhaps. Our relationship was short-lived. I'd get home from work each day, and Berrigan would glance over his newspaper and nod, then adjust his glasses and continue to chew his carrot. We began to resent each other, or I, being the only one working, began resenting him for his lack of contribution. My mother was right, I'd secretly tell myself as I laid awake at night, I should have never gotten involved with such a man, a ... a rabbit. One day, I'd had enough. I'd heard from a girlfriend that an aunt had a friend who kept rabbits in a place far outside the city that would likely take him in. That was enough for me. One Saturday, early, we woke and did ourselves up: I wore my favourite dress, fixed my hair and makeup, and Berrigan donned a suit and his cravat. We spent several hours on the Sarmiento train headed west into the interior of the province. Berrigan was upset. The train was packed. He didn't like crowds—neither did I, for that matter—and there were so many people that for half of the ride we'd had to hold our arms above our heads. When the doors had opened briefly, there was room, so we stretched them into the air and were unable to lower them before the next crowd of people shoved into the car. By the time it was our stop, they'd become numb, sore, and shaking. We got off, and there was grass. Delighted, Berrigan nibbled on it as we made our way toward the aunt's house, skipping back and forth and making all sorts of odd observations and exclamations. I hadn't seen him so happy in years, and, for a moment, this made me terribly sad. Finally, we arrived at the aunt's house, and she gladly welcomed us in. Berrigan, without a word, jetted straight for the backyard. In the kitchen, one wall was filled to the ceiling with decorative plates and saucers from around the world. Some looked like antiques—fine china—but most were cheap and unattractive, dotted with images of animals, birds, and dogs. We sat outside, the aunt and I, and had tea while Berrigan rustled around in the bushes. The conversation was pleasant enough. When we finished, I was almost sad to leave. I looked out into the yard one last time and watched as Berrigan hopped from behind a small bench, chasing a butterfly. The aunt said she'd take care of getting him over to her neighbour's house.

"Don't you want to say goodbye?" she asked as I stood on the doorstep. I shook my head and left, wondering what to do next. She smiled, as if she knew, like me, that some men, no matter how hard you try, simply can't be domesticated. Years later, I went back to the aunt's house with my friend for a visit. As I was passing through the kitchen to the bathroom, I noticed a plate on the wall with the picture of a rabbit. It looked exactly like him.

~~The Fibers~~

It's there, but I can only see it after looking at it for a long time. But, it's definitely there. It's a sort of reddish or burgundy colour. Only after looking at it for a very long time and, like, letting my eyes unfocus can I see it, so it's there. It really is there, though, but it takes such a long time for me to see it that I question its being there in the first place. Because, I think, is it really there, or is it there because it's taking so long to see it or to look for it, I mean. Like a trick of the eyes. But, after looking at it for such a long time, I was sure it was there, so I touched it. Or I reached out to touch it, then hesitated. What if, even after looking at it for such a long time and being convinced it was there, it wasn't really there at all? So I pulled back a bit, again uncertain if it was really even there at all. After a while, I had to touch it, whether it was there or not, because there was really nothing else at all to do in the room. So I touched it, and it was definitely there. At first, I could hardly feel it because it was so soft. But then I touched it again and could feel that it was really there, so I scraped away at it a little bit. It sat there like nothing had even happened. The more I looked at it there, the more I could see it was all reddish or burgundy coloured. Inside it, I mean, because there was a lot of red around the outside of the sore. But no matter where it was or how it was inside once you saw it, there was definitely a sort of reddish or burgundy colour like wine, perhaps; it was certainly there, and you could see it all after looking there long enough. It was like a string or a fiber. So I said, It's like a sort of fiber there, in the middle of it, inside. Because I was certain after looking at it there for so long that it was a sort of reddish or burgundy fiber inside of it all. They all looked for a long time, and one said, after looking at it for an even longer time than myself, it isn't really there at all. After saying this, he crossed his arms and leaned back, if you can believe it, like it wasn't even there at all. I was greatly upset because it really was there. I knew it was. Anybody could see it was really there once they'd had a proper look at it. So I said, but maybe you need to look at it for a long time—even longer. And they said, No, I looked at it for a long time, and it isn't really there at all. I can see, and there's nothing inside it at all. But what about you, I asked another who'd been standing behind me in silence. And he said, Well, not really, no. No what? I asked. It isn't really even there, he said. But it is there, I replied; you can see it inside there. Look, it's right there, I said, a sort of reddish or burgundy. But no, he said, I don't think it's really there at all. So, for everyone else but me, it was like it wasn't even really there at all. Even if they looked at it for a long time. Even though they looked for as long as I did and even longer. When they touched it, it was like nothing had even happened at all, like it wasn't even there. I tried to convince them that if they'd only look a little longer, they'd see that it really was there—some sort of reddish or burgundy fiber, poking out just a little from inside the sore. I held it up in the light and thrust it toward them, pleading. But each one simply shook their head, saying, almost to themselves more than me, as they filed out one by one, We just don't see it; it isn't really there at all.

They have given me a set of tweezers, so convinced they are of the lack of there being anything there that they left them right in front of us. We pick them up off the bed, then, fumbling, place them between our fingers and dig inside of it a bit to find the fibers or whatever's there. We can see it—a sort of reddish or burgundy that's right inside, in the middle of it. On the outside, it's still red and dry and flaky, not fully healed, making it tender on the border of the scab, or sore, or what have you. But the tweezers have no problem locating the fibers once we've placed them inside. How blind these idiots are—they aren't even able to see there's really, definitely something there. Perhaps one or two of them need to get their eyes checked. But really, it's right there. I ease it out onto the bedspread with the tweezers, and it flakes apart into little pieces. Right there in front of us, a reddish or burgundy sort of colour, all flaked out onto the bed in the light for all to see. If only we could pull forth something more substantial, perhaps a longer fiber, intact—one that didn't crumble. They've given me a jar to collect the samples. They promise to send it out for analysis. But due to the lack of agreement on there being anything there in the first place, I'm reluctant to take them at their word.

I've managed to extract a more substantial specimen, a fiber. It definitely bears a sort of reddish or burgundy colour, the same it's had since the onset of our illness, even more so when one looks at it closely under the light. This, now, they can't deny. It's there. For the past several hours, we've teased it out of the affected area slowly. Fragile as the fibers are, I've had to extract them very slowly, teasing them out from the inside a millimeter at a time. I've remained completely still. Once I have extracted a sizable length, there will be no doubt that I've been afflicted. They won't be able to deny it. Then, only once they realize that there's really something there can the healing begin.

It's these things, I keep repeating over and over again, the sores and the fibers that are making everything so painful. If you only looked for a long enough time, you'd see they're really, definitely there, all reddish and sort of burgundy. Dedicate an hour or two to focusing on what's in front of you—on your patient, your comrade, your once-friend. At times, it feels as if they're filling my whole body up—the fibers, I mean. Like they're nearly bursting forth, as if our affliction were more of a blessing than curse, a brimming over of sorts.

I am not possessed. I am dispossessed, having been robbed of the legitimacy of the afflicted. Can you not see it? I ask again, in a voice as hoarse as a whisper. A nurse has just entered to change the linen. Can you not see that it's there? But no, she neither looks nor answers, content with the heavy silence in the room my pleas bed down upon. At one point, she brushes away the flakes on the bed in front of us with the back of her hand in a look of disgust, as if they were crushed bedbugs, as if they were really there. See, I screamed; they're right there. She looks and says nothing, then retreats to the safety of the room's exterior.

Now they no longer bother to enter, those colleagues whom I'm trying to convince. But I continue to speak to them as if they too are there, right beside me. I say colleagues, for are we not both dedicated to the search for truth? I, to prove that something's really there, and yourselves, for a broader form of study—perhaps myself. Please use my affliction as an example to help others see the interior truth. Our food enters each day through a tiny chute in the wall near where we tied the first of the fibers we extracted. There, next to the doorknob, is a sort of greyish nail or screw. It's there where we were able to find an answer, or something more substantial, rather. It's a steel nail or screwhead poking out. Once we located it, after some hours, we managed to extract a substantial fiber, enough to carefully tie around the protruding nail or screwhead. Enough to begin slowly pulling it out of ourselves. Anchored there in the corner, we began to sort of pull it out of ourselves, much like a rogue thread in a piece of clothing. Look, now you can really see it, spread out there from the corner across the ceiling with the rest of them. Look up there, and you can see them all crossing themselves, glinting a reddish burgundy, almost orange, in the fluorescent light from high above. Upon closer inspection, for we had time, there appeared to be steel-grey screw heads located throughout the room. These we've used to create a web out of the fibers. It's actually quite beautiful, even in desperation. They can't deny it's there now. Are they watching the way it sways up there? You can see it; when the food comes and there's a momentary movement, even the slightest, it undulates like a web in a soft breeze. We pass the time with a stillness, looking between its threads, the web, and how even now, even after so much time and effort, it's there, connected to us. How beautiful, we think, that it's really there inside and out, spun and woven. A net to catch the light. Illuminated. It's there, even if there's nobody here to see it but us. Our affliction glints. Another sort of pleading.

What about here? An anonymous man with anonymous features points to the room. Wasn't there something there, he says. His colleagues appear at his side. No no, one says, there's nothing there at all. But wasn't there something in there, I mean? His colleagues line up behind him, forming a line that extends down the hallway. I'm sure there was something there, the man says. Another pushes his way to the front of the line and speaks loudly, in a clear voice. Well, to be sure if there was something there or not, shouldn't we open it? This elicits grunts of agreement that echo down the line. Open it, you say, and the first man says, Yes, perhaps you're right. Perhaps that's the only way we'll be able to know for certain if something's really there or not. But maybe, another voice pipes in, we can see if something's really there by looking through the window. Ah, the first man says, a capital idea. The man then approaches the door more closely and unfastens the latch from a white metal flap covering the window. He peers inside. He clears his throat, then says loudly, There's really nothing there. Really, shouts an anonymous person from the back of the line. Is there really nothing there at all, the man shouts again. Yes, it doesn't seem like there's anything there. Was there something there at one point? What was there then, someone else shouts. I'm asking if there used to be anything there, the first man says a little louder. He raises his voice. Does anybody remember there being something there at one point? This elicits another series of exclamations down the line, then a tepid silence. Well, perhaps, let's take a look inside. That's the key there, a voice interjects. The first man holds the key up, which glints briefly in the fluorescent light of the hallway. Yes, I've got the key right here; shall I open it. Grunts of agreement echo and bounce off the walls. The first man makes his way slowly to the door. But what if there's really something in there, someone shouts. What if it's dangerous? The first man pauses briefly, then waves his hand through the air and inserts the key into the lock, turns the knob, and enters. The rest of them in the hallway squeeze behind him for a look and push him gently through the doorway into the room. See, there's nothing there. Are you certain? Another pushes his way through the crowd and enters the room, standing beside the first. I could've sworn there was something in here. The first gestures theatrically towards the empty room in front of them. See, there's nothing in here—nothing really at all save for a few burnt-out light bulbs and a dirty single bed. The second man gazes, looking from one corner to another. He begins nodding in agreement but stops suddenly. His eyes squint. But what about that there, he says to the first man. Over there in the corner, there's something there. The first man squints as well, then walks over to the corner. Yes, you're right. What is it, he says. It's a smear or flakes or something, the other one says, bending down. It's a sort of reddish or burgundy colour. The first man squats to inspect it. But it's really nothing, isn't it? There's definitely some-thing there, the other says. Yes, but not like we thought. No, not like what we thought, the other agrees. You can see it's there, can't you, a sort of reddish or burgundy, like wine or dried blood. But really, it's nothing, the first one says. I suppose not. No, there's really nothing there at all.

The Line (the Guards & the Men Upstairs)

In front of me stands a man who looks exactly like I do. Behind me is another man who looks exactly like myself. In fact, stretching before and behind me, as far as the eye can see, are men who all bear identical features. The line moves slowly, excruciatingly so. Since we've been here, we have inched forward only three times. Occasionally, other men who look like us pass by to ensure we remain as we are, in the line. They are armed and wear different clothing. We can hardly remember a day that has passed where we weren't standing in this line, wondering what's ahead. It's been so long that we've forgotten—likely all of us—what lies behind us, having passed it so long ago. We must have passed something at one point, but all we can remember is the line. There must have been movement, a history, for we are where we are. All of us, I mean. But for the very life of me—of us—we can't remember. But surely men are not born in a line. Are men born in a line? I shout. The me behind myself elbows me in the ribs, urging silence so as not to attract the guards. The me in front of myself glares at me, as if he's somehow better than me. I open my mouth to respond, but I feel a firm hand on my shoulder. I turn around to see myself, dressed in olive fatigues, with a face like ice. Ah, I say, I could just—but before I can finish, he raises the butt of the gun and drives it into our shoulder, bringing us to our knees. Shut up, I say to myself, then continue on down the line. I look up to my comrades in protest, but I—they—remain silent. I wonder if we were trained—I mean, the guards. Probably not, I think. Probably just slapped a uniform on us. I'm fed up with standing in this bloody line. It is said that the lines in which we wait are vast and imperceptible at times. Excuse me, I ask myself (the one in front) but am elbowed in the ribs. Undeterred, I continue. Do you have any idea why we're—I'm cut off by a more jarring blow now from the butt of my very own (man in uniform) rifle. The sky is so grey it's hardly worth mentioning.

The Guards

I have spent an entire day shooting myself in the face. In all honesty, I've only shot myself in the face once or twice, but once is enough to make the hours extend themselves into excruciatingly long blocks of time. For example, when I relieve myself, all I can think about is my penis as an extension of my arm, shooting me in the face. The face reflected back at me in the mirror while I wash is not my face at that moment in time, but the horrible, confused grimace I bore when I shot myself in the face not hours earlier. It is for this reason that these days are long. At least you're not the one being shot, you say. But aren't I? The soap dispenser shoots its foamy liquid and we, ourselves, in the face. We exit the bathroom, say hello to numbers 1-12 in reception, then exit the guard building and position ourselves in our assigned segment of the line, where one of us is beginning to get agitated. After so many years, we can all tell the ones on edge by a glance. Sweet Christ, I think. I jam myself in the ribs with the butt of my rifle, hoping to nip it in the bud quickly. I (they) open my mouth to protest but think better of it, and we're satisfied, momentarily, striding off in the direction of the horizon. Somewhere far in the distance, a shot echoes, bouncing between the mountainous treetops.

The Men Upstairs

What do we want for lunch? What we always get, number 35 says, we all like the same thing. Shouldn't we try something different, I wonder. We keep this thought to ourselves. Nobody's up for promotion yet. We are the firebrands, the best of our kind. But to try something different—no. Unity begets vigour. Cultured among the rest of our kind in a vacuum, there's not much else we can do. Where we go is always met by similar faces. I know how I will greet myself each morning, devoid of mystery. Team 1 is everybody who was born yesterday; when the next shift changes, it'll be the ones created the day before that. There are drones that look like us but are much smaller; God only knows why. They handle all the coffee runs. Our assignment is to monitor the line and if any one of us takes a step too far in the wrong direction, we're tasked with the terrible. The guards often do what they like, but they still need orders. The only comfort is knowing what our next move will be. Down below, the landscape—the never-ending line of ourselves—bears a striking resemblance to the canal of our palm. We trace it with our fingertip and look there, then out again. A spot just barely catches the light before the line snakes around a corner. Call it in, someone says and elbows me in the ribs as they pass our console. Call it in now. I do, and the dot disappears, like a blip on radar. Much farther back, we shuffle ourselves forward a few more inches—

The Consumption of the Vessel Sarah

It's done, and again, it's as if everything has been made clear, when previously there was a skein between our senses and the full multitude of reality. It's like the film that builds up upon the eyelids of the blind being sliced away. Now I have complete control. The arms. The legs. The smallest fingers do what I tell them to. Quietly, of course. Touch this or that, I think in command, and then they do. They touch it or feel it, and finally, there's a way to assess and analyze such data. We're where the feeling moves up and down and then settles. In front of me shines the booth in which we travel, and everything looks hyper-real, nearly blinding and so brilliant we have to hold a hand in front of our eyes to see. After our eyes adjust we realize that our blindness is due to an increased ability to see into the depths of things, all the way, until the end. To see so profoundly banishes any sense of lingering guilt regarding the consumption of the vessel Sarah.

Our mother is here, and she asks us how we're feeling. I tell her that Sarah is feeling fine. Sarah is feeling much better than yesterday, and we're sure, we tell her, that tomorrow Sarah will be feeling better than that. This prediction, we think, will likely come to pass, as each passing day brings increased clarity and togetherness. Sarah wants something sweet, we say, and our mother smiles, expecting as much. She reaches into her jacket pocket and extracts a bar of chocolate that we snatch away rapidly to consume, but the taste disgusts us. Our mother has to call to have it cleaned up. I've lost complete control. The dirty chocolate looks like shit. Sarah is so very sorry, we say, covering our hands with our face.

This is what I told them: There's not much we can do for her. We've run every physical and psychological test that exists and come up empty-handed, but, as you can see, there's certainly something wrong. It's like all of her joints and muscles contracted simultaneously and locked into place. She's been curled up like a ball for nearly a week.

It is incredibly exhausting to navigate the rocky terrain of the long list of Sarah's feels. It is at times unbearable for us, constantly being tasked with conjuring up other feels for Sarah, strong enough to counteract her more extreme feels. It requires a certain amount of finesse. The landscape of Sarah's feels stretches out imperceptibly; everything is felt with sharp intent. When Sarah feels, the imagery judders on the horizon like a flame being extinguished, but it's never enough to see the distant features. Perhaps this is our primary concern in mastering Sarah's feels: the judder of their hooves.

Immediately after some kind of flash—I don't know, a gun or maybe the Maglite popped, and this cop—sorry, deputy—is flying through the air and smacks against the wall on the other side of the room. The other deputy draws his gun and fucking shoots her. I try to pull him back so he doesn't put another bullet in her. He fucking shoots our little girl, and she drops to her knees. Everyone is screaming, and my eyes are burning from the gunpowder. Then we all stop screaming at the same moment. Beneath all that chaos, you could just barely hear the voice of a little girl, and she sounded happy. After that, I'm not entirely sure what happened. The second officer's light went out, and when the lights came back on, they were gone. She was shaking her head and kept saying it was an accident. We made a mistake—that's what she said, over and over again. Who's we, honey? I asked.

I am Sarah. This, I know, is a matter of fact. I can feel myself even now. But it's like I've been split in half. There is another part of me that's not quite me, and it's slowly dematerializing, but I'm unable to articulate it. When I try to describe it, everything I say is utterly imprecise. Can you imagine being haunted by something that defies description? When someone asks Sarah what is wrong, the only reply I can give is that I'm an overripe pear. It gets worse every day. I find myself in front of the mirror in a daze without remembering how I got there. When I go to switch off the light, I miss and punch a hole into the drywall, and it's blue, like punching through an eggshell. I extract my arm and exit without turning to see if it hasn't dematerialized as well.

The banging is becoming louder and more frantic. Sarah is fine, we scream to whoever's on the other side of the door, Sarah just wants to be left alone. For a moment, there is silence, then the banging begins with renewed fervour. We are soaking wet in front of the mirror. Mother screams, We only want to help you, Sarah, and we reply that Sarah doesn't need your help or anybody's. Sarah only wants to practice her movements. We refill the glass and bring it slowly toward our mouth, but it misses our face entirely. The water soaks into our shoulders, and I'm furious. I move my arm back, and with all her strength, she resists. After a few seconds, we strike the mirror hard with our fist. We watch it darken with our blood, and then the moment descends where we have to take control completely, so we do. We tell our mother we're not feeling well, but it's all right; we'll be out shortly. This calms her. Our mother leaves a second later, and we hear her footsteps echo down the hallway. There are items in the cabinet with which to treat our wounds, so we treat them, then unlock the door and find our way slowly down the hall to Sarah's room. Once inside, our legs buckle, and we collapse.

I swear to God, it's as if I've never seen a day so beautiful. There are so many places like this. I mean, *exactly* like this: as if nothing but yourself exists, which is the way I feel right now. Only you, nothing else. Even the air is different, like a painting that's familiar but indescribable. I want to escape and become a part of everything here, like the sidewalk in front of me. How unexpected, I think. Ahead, there's a shimmering in the air that's beckoning us forward, drawing us to it.

There's a song sung by them about a ship in troubled waters. Do you know it? You do not know it. Belief is the hardest obstacle—belief in anything—a trick really. The very last of it all—love, desire, friendship, what makes up good and evil—all small battles. Our vessel bobs gently in this diary of annihilation, of failures and triumphs; false experience. At times, we wish we didn't need her. We could just walk her off a bridge into dawn's crisp air.

Sarah, we're very worried about you. Why don't you let us see? Because it's not something—see, *mother?*—inside. That's exactly how she said it. I don't understand; what's inside of you? For a moment, there's silence, then a low thumping, like footsteps. But the sound—this thumping—doesn't rise in intensity, come closer like it should if our daughter is walking across the room to open the door. She's a stomper. The sound stays somewhere inside the wall or thereabouts; it's weak and trapped and trying to get out. In another second, I give the okay, and the deputy breaks the door down. The room is completely dark. I stop to let my eyes adjust, but he throws a Maglite on, and there's our baby girl, in the corner by the bed, slamming her head into the wall over and over like she's in a trance.

It is, in some ways, like sliding on a glove. Quite simply. Like sliding on a glove. But when there's a clenched fist, it becomes something else entirely. Like sliding on a glove when there's a clenched fist, which never goes quite simply. These are all learnings. Or no, learning processes. Yes, we are learning, and learning is a process. Another thing like sliding on a glove. But glove—call her Sarah—this glove is a clenched fist. It is the legs of a spider balled up on the windowsill. It is a guardian of something we have yet to discern. A discovery, perhaps, that awaits us once we've locked our fingers in place.

I placed a hand over my mouth to stop me from screaming. There was a lot of blood already. Sarah, honey, one of the deputies says, we need you to stop that. Stop that, she says, in a sweet voice like she has no idea. Her blood's on the wall, and each time she thuds her head against it, she hesitates before pulling it away, and it makes a wet peeling noise I can barely hear over the sound of the blood pumping through my ears. One of the deputies approaches slowly, and she doesn't seem to notice. He's scared and shaking. We all are. He places his hand on her back, and she shrugs it off. All of a sudden, it's as if time has stopped. Hell, maybe it has. I don't know. Can they do that? Then there's a growl, and I'm not sure if it's coming from Sarah or the officer; it's like somebody is trying to speak but can't. Immediately afterwards, there's a flash, and the cop is flying through the air to the other side of the room.

Ahead, there's a shimmering in the air that beckons us forward, drawing us to it. Our vision pulses then goes dark. When we regain consciousness, there's a crowd of people leaning over us, and we feel split in half. But the sky has never seemed so beautiful—so very blue.

▊▊▊▊▊▊▊▊Ward*

First Floor

▊▊▊▊▊▊▊ kept in what appears to be small, glass-like incubation chambers.

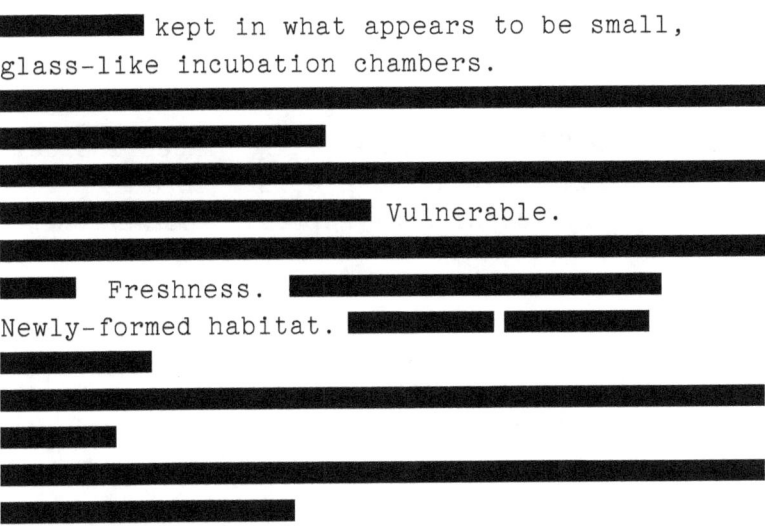

▊▊▊▊▊▊▊▊▊▊▊▊▊▊▊▊▊▊▊ Vulnerable.

▊▊▊▊ Freshness. ▊▊▊▊▊▊▊▊▊▊▊▊
Newly-formed habitat. ▊▊▊▊▊ ▊▊▊▊

---

* The first part of the document was redacted by our agent before being filed, which is unusual but not altogether unheard of. Unbeknownst to him, he may have actually been doing us a favour. We all know which Ward this operative and the ones that follow are speaking of,

██████small, white tube connecting to an exterior ██████ the bellows-like device attached to the center of the bodies. Other wires are fastened at various intervals, likely monitoring ███████████████vitals██████interior mechanisms. Due to limited access ████████ unable to determine with precise accuracy the ██████████ These chambers could be administering the elements necessary to create an artificial atmosphere—construct the optimal environment for cell regeneration. ██████████ RapidX █████████████████ biological ███████████ growth ████████████████ ███████████

██████████████████████████ ██████ speed the process of resistance.

It appears as though they don't excise specimens bearing genetic imperfections. The interior atmosphere—it just now occurred to us—could also be a method of scouring their pink exterior, toughening it before their release. ██████████ if before being placed inside their chambers they've been boiled in a sulfuric solution of some sort. In ████████████

---

but we thought it best to leave everything as is to demonstrate both the mental state and full breadth of the incident. Unfortunately, all we know about the incident is what we managed to salvage before the link deteriorated. We must learn all we can from this so it's never allowed to happen again. Not once throughout our history has such a catastrophe occurred. We are responsible not only for the destruction of countless lives but also for opening a dangerous rift that we're told will take decades, if not centuries, to close, all the while we, ourselves, are leaking through that horrible tear into the unknown. In many cases, we have now become the observed rather than the observer. Although we can't be entirely certain because our connection was severed before we could pull out any of our personnel, there was a fusing of sorts so seamless as to only subtly disrupt the narrative of the event.

places ██████ pieces of their exterior have ████████████████ hardened ██████ flaked onto the bedding of their tubes, leading the observer to infer that ██████████

████████████████████████████ ████████████████████████████ generative cycle.

Second Floor**

Unlike the first floor, which bears multitudes of their young, the second floor is ... Excuse us, we have minimal time to compensate with each shift, and as such, it's rather difficult to be as expansive as we'd like to be. The second floor, unlike the first that was scattered with what appeared to be freshly hatched biological specimens bearing genetic abnormalities, is ... Again, we've experienced a lapse. These somewhat disorienting episodes seem to have increased in frequency since the outset of our observation period, likely due to a slight oversight in spatial calculations or the temporal resistance often experienced by ... Again ... We have to say, collecting data in this environment is excruciatingly difficult and frustrating, but there is no other choice for ... the room lined with beds, and each

---

**Visual transcriptionist's note: at this juncture, the myopic recording shorts out, and we're forced to rely on what Person 0007B gathered in regards to audio only, meaning we're unable to verify the visual truth of their account. Due to the sensitivity of this report and the nature of the accident, the panel would be at a disadvantage to discount this knowledge, as well as that of the myopic technology at our disposal in general, which, of course, as you know, boasts certain drawbacks, the first being the difficulty of seeing items at any distance further than several cosmometers, making any horizontal determinations highly suspect.

ballooned specimen pushed up against the glistening wall ... We have limited time in this atmosphere before the ocular implant dissolves completely, which is also, of course, the cause of this somewhat erratic notation. In many instances, the observer is at the will of the recording device, for it often roams. A tubular chamber extends from the womb of these creatures every so often, extracting fluid, likely in an effort to prevent the drowning of ...

Third Floor

They fold as if mountains: inwards and together, exhibiting a biting malleability somewhat stunning in contrast to what we've seen prior. Our previous assignments never afforded so much insight; rather, they were wayward missions, one might say, half-finished thoughts from our addled superiors—perhaps too strong a descriptor, but we were told never to retract a statement and strive for brevity;it's in our blood. Before the door closes and we're forced to float here and wait for what seems like another millennium, these horrible fleshly creatures that look like folding and melting express themselves fluidically and without restraint; it's a shame they've got us all stuck in this vortex. Some might say our talent's wasting away; at least when they unhook those bloated hags from the placenta pumps on the second floor, they're allowed to go back out again. What would they make of it

if we just left the glasses here and struck out
upon the Cosmic Highway? What then? You'll see,
that's what.
Is this what serves as a "resignation letter"?
It's something one of them described, but her
words were muffled by her chin.

The Village of the Sun

We'd travelled through the barren landscape for a forgotten number of weeks, guided by the subtle glow on the horizon. All our communication equipment was trashed. We were on Earth— we knew that much—so we'd reached our destination, but precisely where on the planet was a mystery. We'd been tasked with finding a sign of civilization, although we knew it wasn't likely, the planet having long since been destroyed by years of pollution, wars, pandemics, and other atrocities often following in humanity's wake.

The air, filled with a flaky, black detritus, at times felt as if one had to swim through it. Our suits kept out anything harmful, but without any protection, no one was bound to make it far in that atmosphere. We continued on foot—without choice—walking over hills and valleys absent of any growth, just hardpan, like Mars before it was terraformed. Our small, collapsible tents fit into our pockets, outfitted with biofilters. Since all the monitoring equipment had been damaged, we agreed that it was best to sleep in our suits.

I awoke late one night to a familiar beeping, alerting me that it was time to empty my sack. It was unadvised, in any exploratory situation, to remove our suits for any reason, so we'd been outfitted with a fine catheter to our urethra and a tubular suction device attached to our anus to collect waste; when the sack was full, we received an alert. If it wasn't flushed within a quarter of an hour, we ran a chance of having it burst—an unpleasant scenario to say the least.

I rose and left my tent. At times, we had no choice but to discharge ourselves while travelling in front of our companions. I still preferred to empty my sack in private whenever possible. Remnants of rubble and asphalt paved a straight line to the top of a small hill overlooking the valley below, deserted save for our meager campsite. Once there, I popped the latch on my left arm and pressed a blinking red button on the control panel, then felt a brief whoosh and heard a faint swishing noise through my helmet. Done, I had begun to descend when a faint glow emanating from beyond the valley caught my attention. It was far off in the distance, perhaps hundreds of kilometers. I quickly woke up the rest of the team, who followed me up the little hill and confirmed what I saw. There was indeed a faint glow somewhere off in the distance—a form of life or a remnant of civilization.

Daylight soon broke. The glow dissipated until it could no longer be seen at all, the sun's haze filtering through the dark miasma and overpowering everything else. We decided from that point on that we'd travel only at night, following the glow. Days passed, or nights rather, and as we grew closer, the glow intensified, until we judged it only several days away. At this point, even during the hazy afternoons, we could make out the faint white radiance on the horizon. It gave us hope, although, of what, none could say. Once visible during the daytime, we travelled continuously, following the glow, drawn to it. There was no need to stop; our suits had been outfitted for every possible scenario and periodically pumped a burst of bio-stimulants, chemicals, and synthetic proteins into our bloodstreams, eliminating the need for rest. Such technology, of course, was designated strictly for high-risk scenarios, but we all felt an urgency, thus we pumped ourselves more and more full of the thwack, as it was called, clattering across the hardpan at an increasingly rapid pace.

It was night when we finally reached the light source.

We came upon a steep hill which took several hours of stumbling to navigate—the rock and sand clipping beneath our boots—then mounted a ridge, staring down onto the glow that had been pulling us towards it all these days and nights. In the middle of it, a kilometer or so away, was a figure. The glow blinded us at first, so we switched our visual filters to dark mode. The land looked like it had been blown apart—a blast zone—burn marks emanated from the corpse or whatever it was; rays reaching out-wards formed a circular circumference around the being, like a bomb that had been dropped. I glanced at my compatriots, who seemed just as dumbfounded as I. There was nothing left to do but descend.

As soon as we stepped over the rim of the deep valley, or crater perhaps more accurately describes it, the glow ceased, forcing us again to switch visor filters. Eventually, we reached the being at the epicenter; it sat before us, clutching a dark black orb in its lap. I walked up to it. My presence disturbed the air in such a manner that the being slowly crumbled, breaking apart and drifting up into the air to join the rest of the black brume floating around us. I gazed at the orb it had held—all that remained—compelled to touch it; a screen flickered, and it came to life.

Orb Transmissions

[the camera angles upon a skinny blond woman seated in the half-lotus position, badly sunburned, blisters and sores upon her skin; where she's seated bears a resemblance to where we stand now—where we've found the orb. We assume, although without complete certainty, she's the owner of the desiccated body that disintegrated into the air moments earlier; she begins to speak]

Sun sana one, we welcome you to this day; for those of you out there watching, thank you for joining me on this journey. Arigato. Welcome. Palms of praise to you, and health and wellness to yours. Now begins the chant in all languages to nourish the body and soul; palms upward, we begin: sol, sola, sul, sale, sole, sola, solea, soil, soleil, soley, solely, solelh, solel, solen, soli, sin, sinne, zin, zon, son, sonn, sunne, sulberi, sulis ...

[it continues for hours, her chanting the word for sun in all languages; at a certain point, one of my comrades suggests I fast forward, and I do so, for a long while, until she places her palms downward; around her, the sky is darkening into dusk; again she turns toward the camera, speaking]

Now it's time we rest our bodies, using the nourishment we've received from the rays to regenerate our cells and heal our souls. Before logging off, I'd like to share with you a bit more of my journey. I've been here for several weeks. At first, I was hounded by skeptics and non-believers. After several weeks of observation, they grew fewer and fewer and one of the yogis—a true believer—suggested I might broadcast my journey for the rest of the world, for those who were interested in experiencing my empowerment.

[at this point, one of my comrades again suggests I fast forward, and I do so until there is only blackness in the orb; I hit play for a few moments, and although no image can be seen onscreen, a steady breathing is heard; after a time, the screen begins to lighten slightly and we see her silhouette, sitting in the same half-lotus position in which she must have slept or meditated through the night; as the sun rises, the same scene from the day before before plays out]

Sun sana two, we welcome you to this day. For those of you watching, thank you for joining with me on this journey; for those who've just tuned in, arigato. Welcome. Palms of praise and health and wellness to you and yours. Now begins the chant in all languages, nourishing body and soul. Palms upward, we begin: sol, sola, sul, sale, sole, sola, solea, soil...

[how much of this is there, we all wonder; there's a data port in the orb and one of us squats down to connect to it, analyzing the data it contains; there are several hundred hours of video; we're baffled about what to do at this point; one of my comrades suggests we bring the orb along and continue to search for signs of life; another argues that we've most certainly found signs of life, referring to the orb, and suggests we return to the site where we crashed to await retrieval; another argues retrieval won't come because we're not generating a general distress signal since all of our equipment was trashed; I suggest we continue reviewing the footage, for although somewhat vague and unintelligible, it remains nonetheless compelling; at this, we all shrug; it's then decided that, for lack of anything else better to do, we will continue to watch the recording; we all huddle around it, seated uncomfortably in our space suits; before pressing play, I fast forward the orb to a random moment in time and again we see the woman, this time, much thinner, almost skeletal; the sun is high in the sky]

Those of you out there on your own journey, following mine, might be wondering about the quality of the body at this point; yesterday, while I was in quiet meditation regenerating from the day's rays, my skin, numb though it is now, began to test me; the sores and blisters that have developed on my face began to burst, dripping moisture down my cheeks and across my lips—I was tempted to stick out my tongue and catch the fluid; just to taste it once, to remember water, although surely it wouldn't have tasted much like the memory of water; you see, I was being tested; such a small thing, to flick out my tongue and catch what fell, but this would have been a betrayal ...

[we watched and listened to the orb transmissions, compelled by a strange urge; perhaps to see her how her journey ended, although surely it could have only ended in death; we sat with her, captivated, watching the sun rise and set; at some point in time I looked up and realized all our sacks had burst]

Sun sana thirty two, welcome to this day. For those of you watching, thank you. Arigato. Much praise; I apologize for the softness of my voice; for those of you joining with me on this journey, I mean, for those who've just tuned in, welcome, palms of praise and health and wellness to you and yours. Now begins the chant in all languages, nourishing body and soul, palms upward, we begin: sol, sola, sul, sale, sole, sola, solea, soil, solea, soil, soleil, soley, solely, solelh, solel, solen, soli, sin, sinne, zin, zon, son, sonn, sunne, sulberi, sulis. suli, sun. Sun sana forty three, arigato. Welcome to the thinness of the air; thank you to all watching and circled around the orb, namaste; I apologize for the swiftness of my voice but time is in the air; thank you all to those just tuning in, fresh palms of praise beneath your feet to nourish body and soil, sol, sol, soleil, soleil, sol, soil, soil, sol, son, son, son, son, sun, sun, sun, zon, zon, zon, zed, zen, son, sonne, sulberi, sulberi, sulis, sulbaris...

[at this point, the picture goes to static; in the dim light from the orb, I see us, huddled, naked, spacesuits cast aside; the black flakes in the air collect around us like moths drawn to the light of the orb's fractured glow; I watch as they collect upon our skin like snow or bits of ash; transmitting again, we watch the orb and resume the chant in all languages to nourish body and soil; sol, sola, sul, sale, sole, sola, solea, soil, soleil, soley, solely, solelh, solel, solen, soli, sin, sinne, zin, zon, son, sonn, sunne, sulberi, sulis; as we chant, the detritus surrounds us in a gyric whorl,

collecting upon our skin; at one point, I look down at my arms
soil, soil, sol, son, son, son, son, sun reflecting the low light in a
dull sheen like the scales of a reptile sonne, sulberi, sulberi, sulis
soil, sol, son lost in the intensity of its stillness, of everything
happening around us; the orb grows dark and there's a piercing
scream from one of our comrades; I'm unable to move, the black
detritus collected upon our skin is now hardened into a crust, and
the air is clear, or we know it's clear, although we're not sure that
it's clear but we can feel that feeling. Before us, the orb begins to
glow: the same dull glow but getting brighter at a rate that's
imperceptible because we're all still lost in that feeling of the air
and of the intensity of it all, still cemented there, unmoving but
feeling overwhelmed; time passes or it doesn't pass or has the
feeling of being disconnected; then the orb rises higher; there's a
feeling of time only because we can see the orb rising; now it's
glowing brighter. The feeling that the air has cleared soon
blossoms into the hardpan of the desert, and we leave our suits
behind us, following the orb with our eyes and feeling it glowing,
getting brighter and growing in blinding intensity until there's a
vibration that begins at the center of the earth, we feel it go
through us, out to somewhere else, and it doesn't stop, it
continues, growing in intensity until the shells on our exterior
begin to vibrate in sync with it, with the vibration all around us;
our black shells continue vibrating as we float up into the air, then
slowly, begin to crack like hardened clay, falling to pieces,
collecting upon the ground below; we're rising, like the orb,
completely lost in the intensity of it all then there's a sort of larger
vibration, music fluttering in the air, weaving through the motion,
through everything; we can't even look at the orb because it's so
bright but we know it's moving, turning around itself in time to
the rhythmic hum, the strange sort of noise echoing all around us;
we're back on our feet now, shielding our eyes from the blinding
rays, and the tension breaks for a moment, surges into the words
of a song and we're standing there, confused, listening to the

melody playing all around us, through our bodies; it's so intense, so impossible; the words of the song—the music— sounding like something we once knew, ages ago, and the words were there with us, so we sang along, chanting about villages, Palmdale, turkey farmers, and hoping the wind didn't blow.

One of my comrades suddenly turns to me, shouting over the din like we're at a rock concert, "So, we're in Palmdale then?"

I am a Blue Person

I am a blue person; there's no doubt about that. As blue as the sky on the brightest of days. As blue as anything that ever was. Quite different from any of my peers, I'm often ostracized for having such a blue take on things. But what can I say? I am a blue person; I cannot act or be anything but. I am the colour of water and the shape of the eyes of a thousand blonde children gazing longingly into the depths of a shallow reverie. My entry into any room is often announced by a series of steady drips, alerting occupants of my presence long before I'm able to find the nerve to speak. When I do, the language is impossibly dense, crowned with useless phrases that haven't been uttered in decades. Tears are not blue but clear, although I've never cried. There is no need, for I am blue. You see, or don't you see? I am smiling, a teardrop in the corner of your eye.

When I was younger, I thought being blue was all about being yellow. It is not. It took me a lifetime to learn that being blue means being blue, not yellow. Being yellow is much different. It is the sunlight, whereas I am the sky. Being blue is more of an afterthought; being yellow is more forceful. Once I'd figured out I was blue, I often dreamt of being yellow—I still do—but now I've accepted my fate. The yellow people of the world certainly do exist, for they are a part of me in the way that the flowers bloom and the plants grow. You see? For I am behind you.

Blending into the background of a variety of settings is not a problem for me. I look great with almost any colour. In fact, I'm often left behind, blended into the wall, the whites of my eyes being the only thing to betray my presence. I overhear many conversations as easily as running water, so it goes without saying that eavesdropping is a favourite pastime. At night, I mix with the shadows, often finding myself in one unsavoury place or another.

What can I say? I am blue; it comes with the territory.

Look behind you; can you see? I am there.

Warmth

I.

"Any way you look at it, it's a helluva circle," he said about the moon. The wind blew like an empty tunnel as we climbed. There was shale everywhere, but no owls. Our boots were made from snakes from Texas.

"Suzy fucked a lumberjack, and then I was born," he said with a snort.

"Oh yeah?"

"Yeahhhh."

"Well, what kinda horse was it?"

"A lumberjack."

He stumbled.

The air up here, you could eat it. You could sell it like ice.

Last year, a fire burned the woods down. It reached all the way to the top of the mountain. Just looks like charred nubs now, dangerous.

"You can see your breath when you whistle," I shouted.

The closer we got to the top, the more the moon made us watch. We ate the horses. They weren't ours, but we ate 'em anyway, even kept the hooves for luck. We used to be dependents, but now we live like free, like this burnt forest. We look dangerous, I bet.

"Hey, you think we look dangerous?" I shouted.
"You bet."

I started feeling real heavy and sat down. I spat on a tumbleweed and watched him sit down too.

This shale is useless. You can't eat it. It's brittle, and it cracks. But you can sharpen knives on it.

I got knives. We both do. I had mine for a long time, and he just got his.

"Hey, you always come up short."
"What?" he shouted against the wind.
"You always come up short," I screamed.
"You're short."

The sky was beginning to glow again. I stood and looked at it. He nudged me. I nodded, then sat back down.

Nubs know no menace.

2.

The sun always wakes us when it's hot. We sleep outside now. Take our clothes off when it's time to get up. Pull the skin off each other's backs while we walk. A home means you're never hungry. Horse hooves aren't lucky, but they'll make a nice ashtray.

"Sometimes I can eat raw meat, and other times it makes me puke?" he spoke. "Because sometimes you have to cook your meat."

I understood.

I always understood big brother best—that's why he's here with me now.

I wake up each morning, pretending I'm something new. He does it too. We pretend we're lizards on the sand, shed our skin. We eat insects. Big brother said we give thanks for the things we named, and this is the way it should be in our minds.

It's winter, but it hasn't snowed in years. Once, I thought I saw snow, but they told me it was only ash.

Soon we'll have to find new furs.

"Tell me why we're here," I said. "Tell me where we've been and where we're going."

"Sit down then."

He squinted out the sunlight.

I smoothed my furs onto the shale and laid down, turning into jerky.

He blew the snot out of his nose, then began:

"In the beginning, there was one star in a pot of darkness. As time passed, the pot began to boil. One day, the pot became full, and the star exploded into everything. That is why we burn but never catch fire. We're part of everything."

"Is everything?"

"Yes."

"Then how come the trees burn?"

"I'm not sure."

"Were we made first?"

"No, we were made long after."

3.

I watched him piss in a waterfall before I did. We stuck the knives between our teeth and went. Things were different. In the water, the fish shine like tin cans, and I can hold my breath for hours. The fish down here are all different shapes and sizes. We catch the ones that glow in the sun like so much gasoline. We eat 'em raw.

Big brother says that back in time, people could become animals. Animals could become people. Spoke the same language. Words like magic. All you had to do was say.

He caught one. We used the shale to scrape the scales off. Ate it raw. Left a cairn of tiny bones on a rock as evidence and started walking. We put our footprints down. They leave marks that no one can read.

Our hair is no longer wet.

"Do we live in a crazy place or inside our minds?"

"Both, I think."

On top of this mountain is another mountain, and another one on top of that. But the wolves won't eat us. The buzzards won't pick our bones. We are them. They are us. One day, the sun will take us back. But now the mountains are much too small. Crow brings us his messages from above, and that is the way things are. No longer can we glide upon the wind, yet our blood burns with it. Our bones were once made of gold.

4.

Hawk says: "Look!"
Eagle says: "Look!"
Fox says: "Look!"
Snake says: "Where?"

5.

The night that father died, the man with the iron face came to our home. He said he had something important for my father and placed a calfskin package on the table. Then it began to rain.

6.

What now becomes the cold big brother?

What now becomes of us? What flows inside our bones? What marrow is ours? Is it fat? Will it burn?

Tell me again where the sun takes us when we die. Tell me again about the place we were before.

Tell me again of father, of mother, of our land whence green. Who shall we pray to now?

Who should we call to fill our mouths with dust?

Who makes the dust of men?

Where is the sun leading us?

Where is the sun leading us?

Where is the sun leading us?

Where is the sun leading us?

Where is the sun leading us?

Squint. Squint harder.

Close your eyes.

Squint again.
Close your eyes.
Eat your dead.

The Contraption (or the Beast in the Boneyard)

- After Theo Jansen

It looked like it had been pulled half-finished out of a dream, monstrous and stripped of flesh. It was gleaming in the early morning sun. With nothing to pick at, we soon began to explore its extremities. After trying for several unsuccessful hours to elicit some sort of response, I slumped down beside it and watched the tide slowly come in. What the hell does it do? I asked the air. Our companion simply looked at us with a blank stare. When we boarded the ferry to bring us here, it was packed. But, little by little, people must have disembarked. We didn't realize it until we were the only two passengers left. When we reached the island, there was nothing else to do but get off. Once we did, the ship disappeared.

After we'd learned to work the bellows, the contraption kept quite a comfortable pace. We decided to pass all of the subsequent days alongside it, walking amidst the tattered remains of cephalopods washed up dead along the shore. It kept the flies off, walking did. We bloat a little more each day beneath the vicious rays of the sun, which haven't ceased since we began this journey. The few seabirds that remain light upon the contraption infrequently, doing so only momentarily, before being scared into the air as it wheezes forward into life. There's a certain rhythm to its movements, which one finds quite pleasing, and the rocks in this locale are relatively soft underfoot.

It has been an eternity, and at this juncture, the glinting of our bones serves as a signal flare into the ether. By now, nearly all our flesh has rotted and sloughed off. There are quite a few more birds that follow us as well. A large amount of time passes before we notice, in the distance, what appears to be a small biplane. We see it when it periodically blocks out the sunlight. It passes between the bones of the contraption; it takes us a moment to realize it's not the shadow of the plane in the distance but the plane itself. We watch it exit the contraption and putter a few hundred meters further down the shore. As we run to catch up to it, I realize the people inside must be terrified.

Exploring Infestation as Art Through Organic Decay

My partner began their creative writing process through practiced bone divination, with the ribs and other bones forming a latticework of scales resonating with each seasoned touch. I was focused on exploring infestation as art through organic decay. It wasn't long before we realized that we weren't at the foot of a mountain after all. The level, windblown prairie that surrounded us was actually the widest brim of the largest hat we'd ever seen. We spent a moment in quiet contemplation and awe, then I sighed, loosening the straps of my travel lab and plopping down into the sand/muck. *With the fading light, it's useless to travel any further,* I said, *hat or not. This seems all right, no? To stop here, I mean.* Without waiting for a reply, I reached among the various spore cultures contained in my travel lab until I found a slug. I chewed it for a moment, holding it in the pocket of my cheek, then spit it out on the dusty/sandy/mucky ground as it inflated. *Take your shoes off this time, all right?* I asked my partner before climbing in. They were still outside, entranced by the colours cast from the bones upon the landscape, which produced something like red bioluminescent flashes that would illuminate everything nearby. It made me think of a pulsar made of blood. We'd been travelling for what seemed like eternity, and everything was dust-covered at this point, the dust being little cosmic bits of detritus, the skin of giants—who knows what else.

It's just before dawn, I think. I'm awake because, at some point, I realized my partner wasn't in the slug and it'd stopped moving. After a time, you grow accustomed to feeling them slide over the uneven, rocky terrain at night. It becomes something you miss when it's not there. I exit and ask, *What are you doing?* Our partner has a chassis bolted around their waist and is wearing the oversized boots used for odd jobs. They're so large that they're crushing everything in their path. *We're supposed to be studying that, you know. Studying what,* they say, frustrated at the slug's indifference. *That!* I point behind us to the path they've crushed through the scrub and organic refuse. *That,* I shout again, *the glop! You stay here and study glop all you want; I'm getting to the top of that mountain today, even if it kills me. Hat,* I shout. *It's a hat.* They glare and stomp their boots hard into the glop. There's a squeaking noise, and something splatters onto the side of the slug. Then they pull out the reduction salt, sprinkle it gently atop its head, and it dries up, away and out of sight. *How many slugs do we have left, anyways? My satchel's full of them,* I lie. That was the last one. *Did we load everything up into the stream already?* I ask them. They simply nod. I look down at my feet at the water running over my boots, and then it recedes, joining the rest of the stream that cuts through the prairie alongside us, tracing an unsure path through the brush as we ourselves did. Then it snaps up like a whip into the air and disappears with

Exploring Infestation as Art Through Organic Decay

everything we've gathered thus far. A pair of giant fingers suddenly blot out the sun. *This is as far as we go, I guess,* I shout as we're brushed off the brim of the hat and into the air. *Ciao, they yell, see you Monday.* We're now free to spend the weekend in whichever manner we please.

Poor Soil

There's a soft thread that binds together permanence and nothingness. This village, twinning with the absence of things: people, lights, the smell of food, and smoke clouding out of chimneys; all the things that give a village life, gone, save for the barren husks of buildings scattered throughout the dust that cloaks the air. We're currently in the world of the living, but only just. We entered the village at night, travelling up the mountain-side into the valley and reaching the gates long after darkness had fallen. They were open wide, despite the lateness of the hour. In the village, there was no light to be seen, save for the weak glow of our oil lamps. The air, hot and humid, was choked with dust. We struggled as we walked, coughing terribly at times, our eyes dry and burning. A drug named Alice, administered with an eyedropper to the tear ducts, brought some small relief; it moistened our eyes and bathed everything in a sullen green glow, eliminating the need for further use of our lamps, which we snuffed out accordingly. We continued quietly, passing one abandoned house after another, their thatched roofs caved in, large portions crumbled away. Stopping to look at one, I kicked a support post; it broke apart like a piece of balsa wood, exploding into a cloud of dirt. The awning it supported quickly collapsed onto the ground, forcing us to dive out of the way to safety. Further down the trail, far off in the distance at an elevation a great deal higher than where we were, we could see a green glow emanating from somewhere off in the forest. Alice guided us toward it, intensifying our experience the closer we got to the septic pallor shining through the trees. In the forest, the air grew even thicker with dust and particulates, leaving a thin film of dirt on our skin. Our partner's appearance gave us a start—it was as if they were covered in mud—and for a moment we stopped and stared. Alice intensified the experience, making them appear as a nightmarish figure that'd risen out of the ground. Suddenly, they began to cough uncontrollably, and a cloud of neon-green dust erupted from their throat, spreading out into the hot night air.

That's the last thing we remember before waking up here.

There's a low glow from a fire in the middle of a dirt floor, casting shadows about the room surrounding us. The walls, draped with animal skins and furs, appear almost translucent, Alice doing her work in a way we've never experienced before, letting us see through our surroundings somehow, out into the thick forest that looms menacingly around the hut, slowly devouring and dissolving the space between the two. Our travelling companion is nowhere to be seen. In the corner of the hut squats an old, broken man, limp skin hanging off his frame like a wet towel. We sense him before we can fully see him. When he notices we've regained consciousness, he scoots his way further into the firelight. For some reason, the more we try to discern the features of his face, the less substantial they are—a sort of dark blemish or smudge where his mouth, nose, and eyes should be. Like the walls around us, he too is draped in various skins and furs, strange medallions eliciting a dull sheen reflected off the firelight. He draws a long, skeletal arm in a sweeping gesture before him; Alice slows down time briefly, exaggerating the motion for added effect. When he begins to speak, his facial features come into focus, and we see that he's blind. His language is unknown to us, but Alice offers a crude translation as he tells his story. At one time, he was the village shaman. Many years ago, perhaps centuries ago, the village thrived, taking sustenance from the lowlands and surrounding valley, farming and raising cattle, fishing, and the like. Then, one year, a powerful drought took it all away. The crops went to rot, all the livestock died, and people began to starve. They then began to call upon the shaman, who'd gone largely unnoticed when times were fair, as is the way of things. One by one, the townspeople came to him for help, and he did what he could, but nothing could bring the animals back, make the crops grow again, or put food in the people's mouths. It was then that he remembered an old spell he'd once read in an ancient book when he was an apprentice in one of the neighbouring villages. After he'd been initiated, he set off for the countryside, helping those he could with his powers. He heard that his old master had died, so he returned to the neighbouring village to pay his respects. His old master had died of a sickness for which there was no cure, or so it was said. Upon his arrival, he was told by an old woman that his master had left all of his belongings to him, which wasn't much—a few rags and a couple of old tomes, one of which he recognized from many years ago. He thanked the woman, loaded his master's old belongings onto his mule, and returned to the village where he was born, constructing a simple hut on the outskirts of town—the one where we now found ourselves. Several years later, he said, the drought hit, and things in the village changed. It was only after he'd tried every means of magic to heal the wounded land and its people that he remembered the spell in the musty old book on his shelf, brought from his master's hut. After flipping through its pages, he came upon the spell and got to work. It was old, powerful magic that threaded the thin line between the magic of the dead and that of the living. The marginalia in the spellbook spoke of the importance of exactitude—one must overlook nothing or else face dire consequences. He soon resigned himself to working the spell and snuck into the village's burial grounds late one evening, scooping up a generous portion of dirt from a fresh grave. To each villager that came to him—for they continued to come—he gave a chicken, which had been raised on a mixture of grain, millet, and the dirt he'd taken from the holy ground. The villagers, he told them, were to roast the chicken in an oven made of mud created from dirt they'd gathered on their property, and then every family member was to eat from it, saving all the bones, which they were to later boil along with a mixture of herbs and spices he gave them. Once this task was done, they were to dry the bones in the sun and then bury them in the yard. One by one, the villagers came and were beside themselves to receive such a meal from the old sorcerer. They followed his directions implicitly. One day, a powerful storm came out of nowhere, and it rained for days on end. Afterward, the plants began to grow again; the villagers bought livestock, and for a time, the village flourished. Although the drought was over, something in the land had changed. The plants grew and the livestock thrived, but the daily chores became a nuisance. Villagers found themselves sweeping more and more each day. Dirt would blow into their homes out of nowhere, and no matter what they did, it remained.

People woke in the morning to find dirt in their hair, all over their bodies, the sheets covered with it. They then returned to the shaman, demanding help. It was then that he realized something must have gone wrong, although he couldn't say precisely what. Things soon went from bad to worse, and many of the villagers took to their beds with a sickness the old man had neither seen nor heard of before. Frantically, he returned to the neighbouring village, demanding someone tell him what had happened to his master. No one would speak to him. At a loss for what else to do, he dug up his master's grave and opened the humble box he'd been buried in, but found nothing inside but dirt. So, the old shaman returned to his native village. When he arrived, the villagers were nowhere to be found. The dirt covered everything. He rushed back to his hut, where a lone man stood waiting for him. The man opened his mouth to speak, but all that came out was dirt, piles and piles of it. The villager collapsed to his knees, then broke apart, and a moment later the wind blew what was left of him out across the fields.

Alice had begun to speak to us once again. Late into the night, we awoke to find the fire nothing more than a few glowing embers, the shaman wheezing in a fitful slumber in the corner of the hut. Cautiously, we crept outside, taking great care not to wake the old man. Once out of the hut, we reached into our pocket and extracted the eyedropper, then applied a generous portion of Alice to each eye. In an instant, everything around us began to glow, thrumming with a vegetative brilliance that was breathtaking in its immensity. Following the brightest path, we traced our way toward another hut off in the distance. It seemed strange we hadn't noticed it before. Its exterior appeared much like the one we'd just left, yet when we entered, the fire took a moment to roar to life. A second later, there was a flickering of light, and the old man emerged out of a darkened corner. It appeared the holographic imaging system had been damaged; his silhouette flickered every so often as he moved toward us, creating a sort of juddering, strobing effect that was quite surreal. He stooped close next to us and said, "Lift my eyelids so I can see you better," so I did, gently lifting the lid of one eye, then the other, until he uttered a grunt of satisfaction. "Tell me about the dream you had," he said, and it was only then that I realized I had indeed had a dream.

I rose in the hut—the prior hut—late into the night. The fire had burnt down to a few smouldering logs and embers, and the ambient lighting was virtually nonexistent. I stumbled outside where it was raining—a torrential downpour. The second I got out of the hut, I immediately sank into the mud. Off in the distance was a yacht with stadium seating. Someone from the top of the bleachers beckoned me to approach, and it was then that I realized it was riding the waves of a river that had overtaken the village, the waters continuing to rise as the storm whipped into a fury. I found myself seated on one of the bleachers, surrounded by several old classmates, and was offered a beer. An awning covered most of the seating area, and we all waited, drinking and watching the muddy waters rise. It was then that I remembered an experience I'd recently had in which I was unable to digitally record a note about a recent dream I'd had. I was explaining to one of my old classmates that, for some reason, every time I'd tried to record this particular note, the digital recording device had only delivered static or had skipped the note altogether, so the files on the recording device would read something like 12-13-14-16 with the number of the particular note in question being entirely absent from the folder. "What was the note—or the dream rather—you were trying to dictate," asked one of my old friends. "It was so strange," I replied, "because I knew it was important, although I couldn't tell you why. There was a sense of urgency. The note—or the dream, rather—went like this: I'm in a classroom where an oversized man is lecturing. On a dissection table lay two halves of a horse's head, the glassy eye of the side nearest me gazing in my direction. For some reason, although I'm unsure as to why, I know it's of the utmost importance that I complete the dissection successfully. I begin cutting, and I find a tiny note inside the horse's ear while attempting to remove the eardrum. I unroll it beneath an adjacent microscope with a pair of tweezers and am both delighted and horrified to learn it's a note from my father, which says:

> *Hello son, I hope you're well. I want to let you know I miss you dearly, and although we can't see each other quite yet, we will very soon. Once you've finished reading this letter, eat it, as it's been soaked in Alice."*

The classmate I was relaying this to made a vague exclamation, and we both looked up in unison to see a giant Clydesdale off in the distance, running down a dock, pulling a shipping container full of mud behind it. It crashed into the water, then tried struggling up the bank for a minute before the weight of the shipping container dragged it down and out of sight."

The old man flickered for a moment, then disappeared without further comment. I retreated out of the hut to find a dozen more abandoned huts surrounding me; of the once bustling village, only huts remained.

In each hut, an old man told roughly the same story about how the villagers met their horrible end. In one, desperate to find my partner so I could leave, I asked where the villagers had gone. The old man scooped up a handful of dirt, let it sift slowly through his fingertips, and gestured vaguely at the space in front of him. Our supply of Alice was running dangerously low, and we frantically applied the rest in hopes of gaining insight into what to do next. The thriving village reappeared, and with the aid of the green paths that went from building to building, we were able to locate the points at which the cursed chicken bones had been buried. The only thing we could think of—the old men were no help here—was to remove the buried bones and perhaps lift the curse. So we did. It must have taken hours, but never once did the sun attempt to rise. In those days, the night itself was an omen that we tried to ignore. We were able to easily see the veins and threads—thanks to Alice—connecting each building to the next. We found an old potato sack behind one of the homes and placed the bones we'd collected inside, along with as much dirt as we could carry, then slung it over our shoulders. We were almost out of sight of the village when we threw the bag of dirt and bones on the ground and quickly rushed back to the front of the village gates. There, we scribbled a hastily written note on a sun-bleached placard we'd encountered by the roadside. POOR SOIL, it said. See, way back when, travellers heeded such warnings and would go elsewhere to settle down. That being done, we returned to our bag of dirt and bones and slung it over our shoulders once again. Perhaps in the neighbouring village, there'd be a shaman who could grow us a new travelling companion. Of course, they'd look a little worse for wear. Christ, we thought—the fading green light of dawn bearing down upon us—if they were ever really there at all.

Self Portrait in the Style of Arcimboldo

First, it's not very well-mounted, always on the edge of a pre-cipice, either looking down or preparing for a long, unending plunge; slow, deep, caressing into whatever lies far below. Fruit for brains (pomegranate, most likely). Well-kept seeds, sweetly wrapped in pulp, sprouting out of the head haphazardly when one begins to speak, flowering into whatever it is they're trying to express. An aphid flies around each—constantly—keeping their growth in check. Bugs for lips, maybe. A forked tongue made out of the finest silver money can buy. A place to stretch away from the canvas at night, to stand still amidst the almost disappearing foreign gestures bouncing off each wall. One leg to stand on, another to dip our toes into. A sphere formed from a substance resembling mercury floats back and forth, monitoring indecision like a level. It's quite obvious when our foundation begins to sink, for all the porcelain beings and objects that have influenced our path in life slide off the brim of our hat onto the floor, causing great echoes throughout the gallery. Eyes—unpolished mirrors. A canteen of butterflies around our neck, a silk thread tied tightly around each finger.

Ooks (Waterproof Radio in the Shape of Lips)

"Ooks, oocks...oosp....oops...oops...opps. Oops! Oopsoopsoops-oops. Oops!" "How do they feel?" "Good, Bert nort perrfect. There's a bit of an adjustment period." That much was obvious, we thought. The tinkerer glared as if he'd heard us actually say this, then forced a smile as he held out his hand. I placed seven pieces of coral in it, and we were on our way, towards where had yet to be decided. Most mornings, we tended to wander until the fresh air caught up with us from the bellows beneath the city. The air wasn't really fresh, of course—around here nothing is—but it still offered a pleasant warm whoosh each morning. When we could find an unoccupied sewer grate to stand over, we'd remain still and let our skirt billow up until we had to press it down again, just like Marilyn Monster. As we crossed the street, one of our cohorts shouted to us. "Nice lips," they said, "you look just like Marilyn Monster." This made our cheeks turn green, and we checked just to make sure we weren't right then standing above a sewer grate with the billowing hot wind flushing up our skirt so all could see what was down below. But we were walking. These new lips—"Oooks," we shouted—"they look pretty good, right?" Out of all the stuff that usually floats down, these lips are probably our favourite. The tinkerer was right though; they do take some getting used to—oopsoopsooops, how hilarious! We're not entirely sure how it works, but things float down from above that can be used in different ways than they were intended. You were probably thinking they're a set of real lips from a real person, haha—no way! Hard plastic, like the shell of a hermit crab. The antenna (it's folding) stretches out around a meter or so when fully extended. There are two dials: one that controls the volume, and another to channel surf. These lips can really groove when they're turned all the way up, but they only pick up a few channels. Speaking, of course, isn't as easy as it sounds. You've got to tune yourself to the radio so the lips can broadcast properly; otherwise it's mostly static.

We soon cross paths with Mariana, and we walk for a time through the crablands to the other end of the marsh, then part ways, explaining to each other that we'd love to see each other more, but these days we simply haven't the time. It is a lie on both our parts, of course. We've never really liked each other to begin with, but a walk is often better with company than alone, especially when the tide is low. Nearby is a rock, and we sit down for a spell, scanning channels to see what we can pick up. The most interesting broadcast is about toy ducks that keep washing up on the shore of some country far away. It reminds me of my lips. There are several others here who have them, which makes them not so unique, more like a fad, really. Keeping up with fashion at the bottom of the sea—or above it, it seems—is no small task. We've left our rock behind, headed toward home now. On the way, we stop in at Jarrod's to pick up some acelga for our mother; she makes the most unimaginable pies. As we wait in line, we fiddle with the knobs of our lips, trying to get it just right before it's our turn. When it finally is, the shopkeeper greets us warmly, and we try to ask for what we need, but all that comes out is static, high-pitched and ear-piercingly loud. The windows crack, then break.

He snatches the lips off our face and shakes his head disapprovingly. Get out, he says. Without any lips, we're unable to protest.

The Armies Ready for War

There are three water bearing taps from which knowledge pours. The water in the first tap tastes delicious even when it's not. Contained in the second tap is an army ready for war, and from the third tap flows a hat you've never liked. There are springs in every town that produce these types of water, but nobody's ever satisfied. Everyone says they know better. So now, there exists everything good and terrible depending on how it tastes, armies ready for war, and the hat-wearing population. Those in the armies ready for war are also fond of hats. A terrible thirst slakes the nation, and hats are growing ever larger to compensate for the vicious rays of the sun. Today the old ones find respite in the fact that, though they thought they'd destroyed everything, they had forgotten about themselves.

My sister and I continue to pick beads off curtains and meta-bolize the plastic they contain, while the rays of the sun grow ever stronger in this knowledgeable, thirst-slaked land. We've tried all the waters, and it's true, nothing works. But everything is beautiful or tries to make sense, which is the heart of knowledge. We watch an army of ants ready to eat a beetle. Like them, they are like us. We are taking a path to town through the hard-walked sand, which I love to walk. The army of ants will still be here. The wars have yet to begin. Life on the brink, I say aloud, stepping slowly, careful not to kill anything. Yet. Everything is an invasion. We finally disappear into the horizon. The sand is moistened nightly, then packed down by tiny steel robots that weigh tons. It is hard, like clay. It's a special kind of steel. To be heavy enough, I mean. The swamp glows before us in the distance. Once we've reached the end of the hard-walked sand, we will each tie a rock around our waist and walk out into the muck.

My sister and I watch the reeds float past. They are dark green too, like everything that passes you while you're sinking to the bottom of a swamp. It's a strange road to have to die to get somewhere. I watch my sister puff out her lips like a blowfish, wondering if it's intentional or not. In a few minutes, she's lifeless, and I'm fading in and out, both of us still sinking. In another moment, I'm out too. When I regain consciousness, she's already dragging her rock behind her towards the rotten clock tower, where the man who holds the keys to the universe resides. We've come to borrow something for our mother. She would have liked to have come too, for she loves to drown herself, but she had more pressing matters and sent us instead on her behalf. Up ahead is a geodesic dome-shaped jungle gym, covered in barnacles. It sank so long ago that it's slowly starting to break apart and float back to the surface. That's no fun.

Once we arrive at the base of the rotten clock tower, I notice there's a notice on the door that says, "Bell broken, please shout." I open my mouth to shout and announce our arrival, but I get a mouthful of swamp water instead. I can hear raucous laughter from somewhere high above. My sister says, *I thought it was a clock tower,* and I say, *What? I said I thought it was a clock tower,* she says, *so why the bell?* I roll my eyes, but I don't think she sees me through the cloudy water. The door to the clock or bell tower or whatever it is grinds open on its rusty hinges, and we enter the mud room, which is really a mud room—like, the definition of mud room was made because someone saw the state of this exact room and said that it could be called nothing else.

The man who holds the keys to the universe greets us and says, *What'll it be this time?* My sister holds out the note our mother gave us, and he snatches it away from her, holding it up to the light for a moment until it falls apart in his hands. *I can't read a goddamn thing,* he says. *This is totally useless,* he says. *How could your mother be so stupid?* he says. I shrug my shoulders, make a 'no clue' face, and look toward my sister, who's puffing her cheeks out like a blowfish again, and this time I know it's not for real. The man who holds the keys to the universe puts a finger in the air—or water—beckoning us to silence for a moment. He floats off into a corner for a brief time, then returns, holding a note, and places it in my hand. *Give this to your mother,* he says. I look at it curiously, but it doesn't look any different than normal paper. *You better go before this one disintegrates too.* My sister elbows me in the ribs, and I begin to shout at her but get another mouthful of swamp water. Isn't this happening to anybody else? I think. Once we're out the door and at the jungle gym, my sister and I place our rocks in the small pile of rocks beside it, which have been placed there for the same purpose by those who came before us for similar reasons. A work crew collects them at night and brings them back to the edge of the swamp for reuse. We watch the pieces of the jungle gym break off and float upwards for a moment before releasing ourselves from our rocks and following their lead. As we slowly ascend, it begins to rain. Silver bullets plunge into the surface of the water, leaving fizzy trails behind them.

Channeling the Plague Wizards

Stellar atoms fell from the sky, mixing with dead skin cells in the air before mutating into little gobs of flesh, which rained in multitudes upon the Earth. Some were said to be large enough to crush people, but that was only rumour, for once the gobs made contact with anything, they exploded harmlessly into a swath of blood. The terrifying rain lasted for weeks, leaving behind a sanguine world that congealed and hardened when the dry heat resumed. Inside the village huts, women gave birth—the infants were quickly consumed for lack of food or buried in forgotten corners, a shame of cowardice against the knife.

A long, red road led to the sea, where the grotto of Lût Pêxember remained hidden during high tide. By day, it could only be reached by submerging oneself and swimming down to the jagged mouth of the cave. At night, the mouth of the cave became just barely visible, and access remained difficult; one had to scale the craggy rocks lining the shore. There were no steps or ladders. When forced to leave on business, Lût Pêxember descended with a rope soaked in oil which he burned afterward.

The grotto contained a variety of chemicals and elemental filings that ceaselessly boiled in large steel pots, casting a dull glow upon the walls. A stone altar containing runnels for sacrificial effluent to flow down into the Earth and worn smooth by centuries stood in the middle of the cave. Lût Pêxember toiled endlessly now, for the rain of flesh had left an ochre tint upon the sea, and the sky darkened more each passing day. When he broke momentarily from his work, he fished or coupled with his beautiful daughters—twins—kept chained in a corner. They were without the gift of speech but had borne him many healthy sons. One of them would give birth to another in a matter of days.

The Necromancer could not remember when his brood first installed themselves in the grotto—centuries, millennia, it seemed—but his daughters remained as beautiful as the day of their interment, Lût Pêxember having mastered incantations to slow the aging process to minuscule proportions. Each week, he sedated the two and washed them with scented oils and perfumes, placing a clean, white dress on each before the elixir wore off.

The rest of his necessities were brought every month by an aging hunchback that kept the Necromancer's asylum a secret out of sheer terror and fear of death.

That morning, as he did every morning, Lût Pêxember walked down to the water that seeped into the base of the grotto and buried his hands in the soft, wet sand, pulling out a thick burlap sack that contained a dozen jars of blood collected from his offspring, bred solely for such purpose. *One more*, he thought.

Channeling the Plague Wizards

Lût Pêxember waited patiently, and when the day finally came, he delivered the child, another boy, and purified it with seawater, afterward drying and wrapping it in a red silk cloth and placing it on a straw pallet next to the altar.

The daughter that had given birth was wailing; the other slept.

Lût Pêxember lit two large torches by the altar.

As he picked up the child, the cloth fell away.

He held it naked by the legs over a large steel bowl, and slit its throat with a ceremonial knife of fine silver and dulled gemstones.

The child's blood poured forth into the bowl and Lût Pêxember held it until the deluge slowed to a trickle, then tossed the exsanguinated newborn away in disgust.

Lût Pêxember set the large steel bowl with the newborn's blood beside the altar, then retrieved the rest of the blood from the Hessian sac, pouring each container into the bowl until all had been emptied. He then set up a tripod, hung the metal bowl from it, and built a fire beneath it, feeding the logs until the contents of the bowl began to steam above the growing flames.

He located the piece of parchment—hidden beneath a pile of rags—that bore the final incantation. Lût Pêxember stood over the altar, reciting the words in a soft whisper, then growing in intensity, only to quiet down again a moment later. He did this for thirteen days and nights while tending the fire, adding herbs and other items to the bowl, stirring it occasionally to ensure the blood didn't coagulate.

After completing the ritual, he let the fire die down slowly and placed the jewelled ceremonial knife in the hot coals. It began to elicit a silver glow.

Lût Pêxember lifted the bowl from the tripod—searing the flesh of his hands but feeling nothing—and raised it high above his head in offering, reciting the incantation once more, then dumped the contents of the bowl onto the altar.

He watched the blood travel the runnels down into the earth.

Lût Pêxember disrobed, fetched a time-beaten wooden bench from the corner and placed it in front of the altar, then picked the ceremonial blade out of the fire, filling the entire grotto with a blinding glow. He then stood aloft on the bench.

With the knife in one hand and his testicles in the other, Lût Pêxember drew the blade across his skin in one swift motion, then held the bloody pouch in his hand like a prize. Again, he felt no pain.

Blood poured from his lower body, mixing with the rest already travelling into the earth below. He stood there bleeding as long as was required for the ritual, then held the hot knife to his wound. The smell of burning flesh filled the air, and the light from the blade soon faded and was gone.

Lût Pêxember sedated his daughters with an elixir brought by the hunchback each month, forcing down their throats a heavy grog of liquor mixed with herbs designed to paralyze the muscles and numb the senses. When they became unresponsive, he built the fire back up and took one of the torches standing by the altar, installing it near where his daughters lay. Lût Pêxember then held his testicles up into the light, detaching one from the other with a sharp eagle's claw worn around his neck.

He approached his first daughter, raising her dress up to her thighs until her sex was exposed.

Lût Pêxember took the testicle in his left hand and worked it inside her womb, then stitched up her maidenhood with rough twine. He did the same to the other, then tied each of his daughters' legs together.

Afterward, Lût Pêxember collapsed, exhausted, into a heap upon the floor.

He awoke to find that while he slept, the wombs of his daughters had swollen and burst. A large, sickly white grub was visible inside each cavity, feeding upon their dead flesh and rapidly growing in size. Lût Pêxember spent the rest of the day in mourning while the worms fed.

Once they had eaten their fill, the Necromancer began the ablutions of metamorphosis, chanting while the giant worms retreated to the highest corner of the grotto and settled into their cocoons.

Lût Pêxember chanted incessantly into the nights and days until time no longer mattered. When scratching and cracking sounds came from up above and the creatures fell down onto the grotto's floor, he stopped, in awe at his creations.

Before him crawled two chimeras with human limbs and distorted insectile features. They screamed and stretched their wings, then stood on two legs and beheld Lût Pêxember blankly, then each other.

The winged beasts fornicated for a week. When they were done, one creature ate the other, opening its serpentine jaw to accommodate the other being's girth. After its meal, Lût Pêxember gently lifted the engorged creature and walked toward the wall of the grotto where his daughters—now nothing more than bits of bone—had lain, and chained the being up by the leg.

A new brood, he thought.

Days later, while dozing on the dirty floor, Lût Pêxember perceived a vague buzzing noise. It grew in intensity for several minutes until it became a deafening roar. He rushed over to find a swarm of large flies devouring his creation. Soon, no trace was left of their progenitor.

Lût Pêxember threw a mixture of chemicals into the fire—it glowed green momentarily—and the swarm left, travelling close to the top of the grotto, out into the ever-darkening sky.

The fruits of his labours were confirmed several days later by the hunchback, who cautiously guided his skiff through the lagoon to the mouth of the cave and whistled loudly, refusing to come any nearer. Lût Pêxember was forced to stand and strain to hear the man's feverish ravings above the noise of the winds and the sea.

In the village, there was no livestock to speak of, so the swarm spread their wrath upon the townspeople, devouring everyone they found.

After relating the news, the hunchback departed without another word.

Lût Pêxember watched him go until he was just a speck upon the black sea, then retreated inside.

Sometime late in the night, Lût Pêxember awoke in alarm. The grotto was flooding with ruddy water. He looked about his things—old spell books, spent potions, the rusted aftermath of the ritual—and decided there was nothing he couldn't part with.

Hastily, he disrobed and dove into the deepening waters of the grotto, guiding himself toward the cave entrance by sliding his hand along the wall. His powers were formidable, but the Necromancer knew the gods of the sea outweighed them all.

Lût Pêxember was still sliding his fingers along the wall of the submerged grotto when he felt a strange sensation—a tingling in the fingers that grew more pronounced with every movement. It had been centuries since he'd felt a physical sensation; the potions he took extended his lifespan but obliterated all his senses.

Reflexively, he lifted a hand in front of his face but saw nothing.

Lût Pêxember abandoned the idea of guiding himself along the wall and swam as hard and as quickly as he could. The strange sensation spread throughout his body; he sensed himself changing, mutating, soft flesh slipping away, floating upwards, his arms and legs growing longer, more pliant with each stroke.

He reached the entrance to the cave.

Rather than surface, he continued underwater, gliding smoothly, instinctively avoiding the jagged rocks in the direction of the shore surrounding the lagoon.

The Necromancer emerged from the sea onto blackened sand.

The left eye discerned only darkness, no moon, no stars, no sun—absolute blackness, but the right eye gleaned a large, distant, molten flame, indescribable—language, as it was, now annihilated. The Necromancer hopped silently off the black sands, returning to the sea, led by the unshakable force of the amphibious lodestone looping throughout his iron blood.

www.ingramcontent.com/pod-product-compliance
Lightning Source LLC
Chambersburg PA
CBHW051346020726
47501CB00007B/2300